Praise for Melissa Schroeder's
A Little Harmless Pleasure

"This is a melt in your mouth and ask for more story."

~ *Kirra Pierce, Just Erotic Romance Reviews*

"Bravo Ms. Schroeder! I enjoyed your multi-dimensional characters working out lifestyle and love issues. Please quickly work on Evan's story. Can't wait to see this proud Dom fall!"

~ *Victoria, Two Lips Reviews*

"…will make your pulse race and leave you wanting more."

~ *Whim's Place Reviews*

"This is such an exciting read. Oozing with sensuality, Ms. Schroeder artfully describes the scorching heat between these two characters."

~ *Valerie, Love Romances and more*

"This story was hot enough to have steam coming off of it."

~ *Night Owl, Enchanted Ramblings*

"This story is a feast of sexual delights that will have you gulping pitchers of cold drinks."

~ *Candy Cay, Coffee Time Reviews*

"An engaging and entertaining tale, I highly recommend A LITTLE HARMLESS PLEASURE."

~ *Jennifer Bishop, RRTerotic*

"A Little Harmless Pleasure was a great story to follow up A Little Harmless Sex...another delightful story that will have you turning the pages."

~ *Pam, A Romance Review*

Look for these titles by
Melissa Schroeder

Now Available:

Grace Under Pressure
The Seduction of Widow McEwan

A Little Harmless Series:
A Little Harmless Sex (Book 1)
A Little Harmless Pleasure (Book 2)

Once Upon an Accident Series:
The Accidental Countess (Book 1)
Lessons in Seduction (Book 2)

Print Anthology:
Leather and Lace

A Little Harmless Pleasure

Melissa Schroeder

A SAMHAIN PUBLISHING, LTD. publication.

Samhain Publishing, Ltd.
577 Mulberry Street, Suite 1520
Macon, GA 31201
www.samhainpublishing.com

A Little Harmless Pleasure
Copyright © 2008 by Melissa Schroeder
Print ISBN: 978-1-59998-561-9
Digital ISBN: 1-59998-540-3

Editing by Sasha Knight
Cover by Scott Carpenter

First Samhain Publishing, Ltd. electronic publication: February 2008
First Samhain Publishing, Ltd. print publication: December 2008

Dedication

To Jean, reader extraordinaire. You gritted your teeth and showed that bitch Katrina what a real New Orleanais is made of. This one is for you, woman.

Acknowledgment

I would like to thank Stephanie Vaughan for the help in research and encouragement in the writing of this book. Any mistakes made are mine and mine alone.

Author's Note

As a writer, many things inspire me, but this book was difficult. I wanted to tell Cynthia's story, and it just wasn't working. Then, one day I was listening to Keith Urban's *Golden Road* album and my favorite song from the album played, and it all clicked for me. Radney Foster's and Darrell Brown's "Rainin' on Sunday" became the soundtrack to this book. Urban's voice melded with lyrics set to the perfect music. It is about more than love on a rainy Sunday afternoon. It is about saying "to hell with the world" and finding acceptance and surrender with the person you love. At least, that is what it meant to me. And I hope you see that with Cynthia and Chris.

Chapter One

Cynthia dabbed a bit of perfume behind her ears and studied her reflection in the mirror. Pale, underweight, boring. Releasing a sigh, she ordered herself to ignore her inner critic. She reached into her makeup bag and pulled out the pale pink lip gloss, wishing for once she'd gone for the red lipstick she wanted so badly. Again, as she'd done over the past few weeks, she squashed the need to rebel against her upbringing. A Myers woman didn't wear trashy clothes or outlandish makeup. She dressed conservatively, spoke softly, and was probably the dullest person on the face of the earth.

She jumped when a loud rap at her bathroom door brought her out of her thoughts.

"Cynthia."

Anger resonated from her father's voice, penetrating the bathroom door. She cringed and took a deep breath.

"I want to talk to you right now about this nonsense."

She swallowed and looked at herself again. If possible, her face paled even more. Getting past the panic that had her stomach flip-flopping, she screwed up her courage and turned to open the door.

At the age of sixty-five, her father was still considered a handsome man. In excellent shape, with more money than he knew what to do with, he could charm just about any woman into bed, and had on occasion. Her parents had an understanding in their marriage Cynthia couldn't fathom. Her mother had fallen for his good looks and his family background, but Cynthia had witnessed this side of him too often to be charmed. Anger reddened his face and caused his eyes to bulge. His lips turned down in a frown that could scare a gator.

"Cynthia Louisa Myers, I want to know just what the hell you think you're doing."

The urge to slam the door in his face came and went without it ever showing on her face. She'd spent years learning how to hide true emotions. Unfortunately, her ulcer, which her doctor had just informed her about, started to churn in her stomach.

"I'm getting ready to go to Max and Anna's wedding."

There, that was brave. She could handle this. She could do what she wanted without fear. Or without showing it.

"I will not have it." Her father leaned forward, trying to intimidate her with his size. "I've said this before. I don't want you to have any contact with Max and his slut."

Anger pulsed through her. Another shard of pain radiated from her stomach. "I told you not to call her that. And I don't care what you say. They both went out of their way to make sure I knew they wanted me there." And after the way she had almost caused them to break up, Cynthia thought she owed them for their kindness.

Her father's mouth opened and closed, twice. His face flushed an even brighter shade of red. "Young lady, you will do what I say, or—"

"Or what, Father?" Her voice had gone soft. No matter how many times she went through this, no matter how old she was, she reacted like a child when her father confronted her. She hated that she wasn't strong enough to yell back. Hated that even now she wanted to curl herself into a ball and cry.

He schooled his features. His eyes, so much like her own, turned cold. The fury seeped out of his face. When he spoke, his voice was no longer hot with anger. "This is what you want?"

"What I want? When has it ever been about what I wanted?"

His eyes narrowed until just a little of the soft blue of his iris was visible. A shiver skated down her spine and chilled her. "I don't know what the hell your problem is, Cynthia, but I will tell you this. If you decide to do this—if you defy me—you are no longer welcome in this family."

Pain splintered her heart. "What are you saying, Father?" But she knew. Breaking off the engagement had been her one act of defiance. Even though she had tried to get Max back, he'd been lost to her from the time she'd ended the engagement—not that he had ever been hers to begin with. He'd finally acknowledged his feelings for Anna, and there was nothing Cynthia could have done about it. And now there was nothing she would do.

"You were raised to make a good match. And you did with Max, but you fucked that up." She flinched at his unusual use of vulgar language. "I thought maybe we could find you someone else, but you're a laughingstock. Going to the wedding of the man who dumped you for a tramp."

"So, what? Now that you can't sell me, you don't want to have anything to do with me?" She couldn't stop the little catch in her voice.

He pursed his lips before flattening them in a straight line. "I've given you your choices."

He turned without another word and left. His angry footsteps echoed down the hall as he stomped away. She swallowed the hurt and anger, but felt another twinge in her

11

tummy. Before leaving the bathroom, she grabbed up her medicine and took her dose. After downing the pills, she looked at herself in the mirror, squared her shoulders and told herself it didn't matter.

It did, but she wouldn't let it bother her today.

Today, she had a wedding to attend.

Chris Dupree watched Max tie his bowtie as he grinned like a fool.

"You sure you want to do this?" Chris asked, eyeing him with speculation. Max's grin grew wider.

"You've met Anna." He wiggled his eyebrows at Chris, causing Chris to laugh. "And besides, you're looking at a fool in love." Max turned to check out his tux in the full-length mirror. There wasn't much room for anything else in the church's groom's room other than Max and himself.

Chris snorted. "I understand the fool part."

Max flashed a smile at him in the mirror, but said nothing. Chris had been surprised, to say the least, when he met Anna. Bold, beautiful and exactly what Max needed, in Chris's opinion. Just the opposite from what he'd expected Max to choose. As rigid as Chris was laid back, Max needed someone who wouldn't put up with his heavy-handedness. Because Chris wasn't one to suffer fools, the two of them had hit it off almost immediately when they'd met in college. They'd made an odd couple for a friendship, especially on the campus of conservative University of Georgia. Max, the white son of landed Southern aristocracy; and Chris, middle-class kid, the product of a Creole mother and white father, had somehow clicked when they met in their first macroeconomics class. They were sharing an apartment by the end of that semester, both graduated with honors the same semester, and even after Chris relocated to Honolulu, they tended to talk on a regular basis.

"So, is it true your ex-fiancée is going to be here today?"

"Yeah. Anna insisted. Which is amazing, because—well, if you hadn't guessed, she has a bit of a temper." He faced Chris. "But Cynthia smoothed things over at the country club up in Valdosta for Anna. You remember Freddy, don't you?"

Chris nodded, remembering Anna's ex-boyfriend and how their fist fight with him landed both Chris and Max in jail.

"He tried to cause problems for Anna and me. Mainly Anna. He used some of his influence to try and keep her from booking the place for the reception. Cynthia took care of it. She's gone out of her way to make sure everything runs perfectly for the wedding." He paused, and his smile faded. "I just worry about Cynthia a bit."

Max grabbed up the ring box and tossed it to Chris.

"Worry about her?"

For the first time since Chris had arrived, Max frowned. "You know her father, Justin Myers. He's a jackass, thinks women are in two categories—slut and Madonna. And he doesn't think women have any brains. She's been raised to make a good marriage, that's it. So, now that she has defied her father, she's probably close to getting disinherited. And she's...a little fragile."

"Hmm."

A sharp knock sounded at the door. Without waiting for an answer, a petite blonde dressed in a conservative suit walked into the room.

"Cynthia, you could have waited for me to say come in. I

could have been undressed," Max said with a smile.

She looked him up and down. "Not like I haven't seen it before, Max."

Max's jaw went slack and he laughed. "You've been spending too much time with Anna."

She shook her head, freezing when her gaze made contact with Chris. His pulse skipped a beat as they stared at each other. The first thing that struck him was that this woman was so different from Anna. With her smooth blonde hair, her cornflower-blue eyes and her beige, nondescript clothes, she was almost the antithesis of Max's vibrant fiancée. She studied Chris, no expression on her face other than a polite smile that didn't quite reach her eyes.

"Cynthia, this is my friend Chris Dupree. You remember I mentioned him."

"Of course, Mr. Dupree, you're the best man. So nice to meet you."

Did he imagine it, or did her voice just dip lower? It *had* deepened, along with that upper-crust Georgia accent. A flash of heat licked through his blood. Even after all his years in Hawaii, Chris was still a sucker for Southern women.

He stood and offered her his hand. "Nice to meet you too, but please, call me Chris."

Her smile turned real, reaching her eyes. A dimple appeared on either side of her mouth, and her face came alive. She took his hand. The moment they touched, her face flushed pink. He'd never been one for petite blondes, especially ones who blushed, but for some reason he felt a spark of interest.

For a moment, she seemed to hold her breath, her mouth partially open. She looked down at their joined hands and her face turned a brighter shade of pink. She released his hand and stepped back. But she still stared at him, as if he were a forbidden treat she wanted to take a bite out of. His body warmed, even though the A/C was cranked up high. She licked her bottom lip. Chris couldn't help it, his attention snagged on that plump pink tongue swiping across her lower lip.

"Did you come here for a reason, Cynthia?" Max's voice seemed to break the spell.

She blinked, and looked at Max, dismissing Chris. Which annoyed him, for some unknown reason.

"Yes. Your mother and Anna are driving me insane. Anna's mother, thank the good Lord, is the only calm one of the bunch. Your mother asked me three times if you had the ring. Anna said you'd better be ready the moment it's time to walk down that aisle."

"Tell her I promise. And remind her she's the one who's usually late. Is there anything else?"

She shook her head and turned to leave. When she reached the door, she glanced back over her shoulder. "It was very nice to meet you, Mr. Dupree." Her voice was soft and lyrical, reminding him why he'd missed Southern women. When their accent deepened like that, it made it sound as if they'd just had great sex. She slipped out without another word. Chris had to tear his gaze from the closed door back to his host.

Max stared at the door, then looked at him. "You know I tend to mind my own business."

"One of the things I like about you, Max."

Max's eyes narrowed at Chris's dry tone. "Nevertheless, Cynthia is not someone you would be interested in."

He wasn't *that* interested, but he still didn't like Max's insinuation. He didn't want to think the friend who had stood up to more than one bigoted jackass in college would let him down now. "And what does that mean?"

15

Max sighed and muttered something Chris couldn't make out. "I know you, Chris. You lead a certain lifestyle—"

"Not anymore."

Max's eyebrows rose to his hairline. "And when did that stop?"

Chris thought back to Jasmine, his last sub. By the end of their relationship, he wasn't sure he'd ever trust another woman again, let alone trust one enough to commit to a Dom/sub relationship.

"Bad experience. Decided it wasn't for me." He was sick of trying to fit into a lifestyle where he was considered an outcast. Many within the D/s world didn't accept switches, thinking of them the way many people thought of bisexuals. They couldn't understand why someone couldn't choose one role and stick to it. "Don't worry. I won't eat your little Cynthia." Even if the comment conjured up the most delightful imagery.

Frowning, Max tilted his head to one side, studying him. "I don't think you'd intentionally hurt her. I just saw the look you gave her, and I know you."

Chris laughed. "Yeah, and until Anna, you weren't much better. Hell, both of us were pretty bad back in college. But don't worry. I'll be nice to Cynthia, and I promise hands off unless she makes the first move." He thought about those bluer-than-blue eyes and the look she'd given him when she'd seen him initially. "I have a feeling that's not going to happen."

Cynthia sipped her champagne, watching Anna and Max dance their first dance. They looked so happy...so in love.

She squelched the sheer envy that whipped through her at

the sight of the two of them dancing. It was beneath her, especially since she had almost caused them to break up. And, for once in her life, she would not wallow in her own self-pity.

Cynthia sighed. Okay, she felt a little jealous, but that was to be expected. Max and Anna definitely had something very special. When you were in a room with them, you could feel the energy between them, so any red-blooded American girl would be envious. Even after everything, though, she was happy for them. Happy that they had found each other.

Throughout the day, she'd ignored the looks cast her way— some expectant, waiting for a fight; some pitying, thinking her the jilted party. She didn't care. She had other things on her mind. Like being homeless.

"Such a serious expression on such a beautiful face."

She glanced over her shoulder and turned to face Chris Dupree, who was standing just a few feet behind her. Tall, lean, yet well-muscled, with skin the color of mocha, Chris smiled at her, and her knees weakened. He had one of those smiles you could tell would melt the heart of the hardest woman, all teeth, complete with dimples. Add in what looked to be a body made of sinewy muscle, a strong jawline—which Cynthia could never resist—and those twinkling eyes, and the man was Dangerous with a capital D. She'd love to lick him up one side and down the other just to see if he tasted as sweet as he appeared.

Good God. Where had that thought come from? She'd had too much champagne. Or maybe she *had* spent too much time with Anna. There was no other reason for her to be acting this way. She'd never thought herself a bigot, but she'd never even considered dating a black man before. And here she was, contemplating what Chris would taste like. If her father thought breaking her engagement to Max had been embarrassing to the family, he would have a stroke if she dated a black man, no

17

matter how rich he was. Justin Myers came from a good old Southern family, with lots of old Southern money. Just last week she'd heard an aunt refer to the Civil War as the War of Northern Aggression.

She set her empty glass on a nearby table and arched her brow. "Are you having a good time, Mr. Dupree?"

His smile widened. "Are you going to ignore my question?"

Irritation lit through her, but she suppressed the urge to snap at him. It almost overwhelmed her, the need to tell him to go to hell and leave her alone. But twenty-nine years of lessons couldn't be overcome by a little champagne. Besides, Cynthia had been raised not to confront problems. Her mother had always said it was better to smile and work your way around it. But more and more, especially because of the last few weeks, she found it harder to do. Thirty years of training down the drain. Just another symptom of spending time with Anna.

She smiled. "It wasn't exactly a question, Mr. Dupree."

Her voice had turned coy, all of its own accord. His eyes flared, just a bit, and his smile went from genial to seductive. She blinked as her thoughts scattered. A flush of warmth spread to her tummy and then ventured to the rest of her body.

She reached for another glass of champagne.

"I thought you said you would call me Chris."

Ahhh, he had the best voice. Deep, almost poetic, the flavor of New Orleans flowing through it. Each time he talked, she could feel fingers slide down her spine. She took a sip of champagne before answering.

"Sorry. It's just my upbringing."

He chuckled. "Oh, I know all about that, Ms. Cynthia. My mother didn't allow any of her children to show disrespect."

She didn't know what to say to that. Apparently, she'd lost

her ability to hold idle chit-chat, something she'd excelled at just the day before. It was this man's fault. He was smiling at her, talking to her in a voice that promised lazy Sundays in bed.

Oh, bad idea, Cynthia. Don't think about this man and bed. Sex with Chris Dupree was way out of her league. The man oozed sensuality with every move. He looked like a man who knew what he wanted and didn't have a problem going after it. Max was like that. But where Max had made her nervous, Chris made her uncomfortable. Cynthia had a feeling Chris would know how to ease her discomfort, starting with those magnificent hands. Again her face heated as her mind conjured up images of the two of them. What was wrong with her? Hell, she didn't even like the act. And why was she thinking about bedding this man? Or thinking of any man in that area? So what if just the thought of him wearing nothing but that smile made her nipples harden?

She cleared her throat. "Your mother sounds a lot like mine. Max said you grew up in New Orleans, but you live in Honolulu now?"

He nodded, his gaze never leaving her face. Oh Lord, she was babbling. She shifted her feet, trying to ignore the dampness between her thighs. Her panties rubbed against her mound, ratcheting up her tension.

"Do I make you uncomfortable, Ms. Cynthia?" He stretched out her name, emphasizing the "Cyn" part of it. She had to hand it to the man—he knew how to make a woman pant. And drool. She was tempted to wipe her mouth to check.

"Chris, I have an idea that you know exactly what you're making me feel."

His eyes widened in feigned innocence. "You think I'm doing it on purpose?"

She didn't miss the way his eyes skimmed down her body,

pausing briefly in the area of her breasts. He had to know she was turned-on. Her nipples were pressing against her blouse.

"I don't think you do it on purpose. It probably just comes naturally."

He threw back his head and laughed, the sound of it drawing the attention of people close by. Nerves already out of whack stretched thinner, and she drained her glass. She didn't need this stress. It had been a hard few months, and now having a man whom she could never handle flirt with her—it was too much. Not to mention the interested stares of people she knew.

Then the absurdity of the situation hit her. This man wasn't hitting on her. Men like him would never be interested in Cynthia. A bubble of laughter escaped before she could stop it.

"Seems like you two are having a good time."

Cynthia jumped as Max's disapproving voice cut through their laughter. She peeked back over her shoulder and had to fight a giggle. The thunderous expression on his face reminded her of a big brother itching to bust a few heads on her behalf. She would always see him as that, and would have even if they had married. Anna slipped around him and approached Cynthia and Chris.

"Good Lord, we can't have that, Max. We spent a freaking fortune on the reception. People enjoying themselves is something we wouldn't want."

Anna winked at Cynthia. She couldn't help it, she laughed again. When a waiter walked by with another tray of champagne glasses, Cynthia traded her empty one for a full one.

"Anna, Max is right. A Myers does not show enjoyment in public. One might think they were...I don't know..." she said, leaning forward and almost falling down, "*human.*"

She blew a lock of hair out of her eyes and straightened, losing her balance. Stepping back to steady herself, she came up against something very solid, very hard. Her body jumped to life as arousal swept through her. Chris's crisp, clean scent enveloped her senses. For a half a second—okay, a whole second or two—she thought about leaning into him, having his arms wrap around her, feeling his lips brush her ear.

Anna laughed. "I think you should get something to eat, Cynthia."

Cynthia shook her head and pulled away from Chris. If she stayed close to him like that, she would end up embarrassing herself by rubbing up against him. And there was no need for that. She was a Myers. It simply wasn't done. Although it would be really nice to kiss him. His lips were full, sensuous, and Cynthia would bet her newest pair of Jimmy Choos the man would make her bones melt. And she had never been a melty kinda woman.

"I'm fine. Just need to slow down on the champagne." With that announcement, she drained the glass of its contents and slammed it down on a nearby table. Her head wobbled, slightly off balance, as if it were floating about three feet above her body.

"Cynthia, I think you need to sit down." Max's eyes clouded with concern.

She snorted. "I don't need to sit down. I need to dance."

The band began playing another waltz. She grabbed Max's hand. "I'm borrowing your husband, Anna."

Anna laughed as Cynthia led Max to the dance floor and further away from the temptation Chris Dupree presented. Even as lightheaded as she was, she knew her life was beyond complicated. And Chris, with his sinfully beautiful body, was one extra complication she needed to avoid.

21

Chapter Two

Chris watched as Max twirled Cynthia around the floor. His friend had more courage than he did. A woman who appeared to have had nothing to eat, with that much champagne, would not hold on to it for very long. But Max didn't seem to be in control of the situation, which was a little entertaining.

"I guess I shouldn't be so amused, but I can't help it," Anna said with a laugh.

Chris looked down at her and smiled. Again he was struck by just how well Anna suited Max. All through college, Max had been so controlled, and Chris could see how a woman like Anna would loosen Max up.

"You know, if she throws up, she'll be mortified." Anna sighed.

He returned his attention to the dance floor and laughed at the pained expression on Max's face.

"Cynthia comes from a rich, white, Southern family. Of course she'd be mortified."

Her brow wrinkled and she sighed again. "Cynthia takes it to the extreme. It can't be healthy." She sipped her champagne. "I've *never* seen a woman who showed so little emotion. Especially a *Southern* woman. We take emotional outbursts to a whole new level. I consider it an unappreciated art form."

He chuckled. "My mother sure can. Nothing like being cursed in three languages. English, Southern and Creole, my mother uses them all."

Anna's expression lightened, and she shot him a look out of the corner of her eye. "You sound like you're close to your family."

"That's putting it mildly. I'm sure by the time I turn my phone back on, I'll have had at least a dozen calls from my brothers and sisters, and a few from my mother."

"Max said you had a large family."

"Yes, and just like any tight-knit Southern family, it seems like it's twice as large as it really is."

"I was an only child, like Max, so I have no idea what it's like."

His attention went back to Cynthia and Max. "What about Cynthia?"

"Youngest of two. She has an older brother, Randall, who's a real jackass."

"No, really?"

Anna snorted. "Hard to imagine. But, yeah, he's just like her father. Apparently, his parents did little to dissuade him from the notion that he's king of South Georgia. Thankfully, he moved down to Jacksonville, where he is ruling as the king of Northern Florida. But he does show up every now and then to make Cynthia's life hell."

"What do you mean?"

"Well, they aren't happy that she isn't married—the only thing a woman can do, ya know?" Sarcasm laced her words. "He either lets her know she failed the family by not marrying Max, or he brings one of his creepy friends to fix her up with. I know the last one was in his fifties."

The need to find her brother and beat the hell out of him almost choked Chris. He took a drink of his champagne, and the urge lessened a bit, but it still simmered under the surface. It wasn't something he was used to. Yes, where his sisters were concerned he would hurt any man who hurt them, but he had never been particularly possessive of women with whom he was involved. And he wasn't involved with Cynthia. The word "yet" whispered through his mind, but he dismissed it. The woman looked to be a basket case, with too many problems. Pity.

"Oh, thank the good Lord. The song is over." Anna grabbed his hand and tugged him along with her. "We better save the groom and his ex-fiancée. Besides, it's about time for the bride to drag the groom off to have her way with him."

As Max led her away from the dance floor, Cynthia shook her head. Although they had stopped dancing, the room still spun. It had been fun dancing with Max, even if her mind kept drifting back to the tall drink of water with Anna. Of course, it would have been a lot more fun without having Max griping at her.

"And another thing—you shouldn't go so long without eating, Cynthia. You're too skinny by far, and then you drank at least half a bottle of champagne! I'm amazed you can walk without falling on your face."

Irritation crawled down her spine, and this time she didn't repress it. When they reached Anna and Chris, she let loose. Turning toward Max, she shot him a dirty look. Apparently the look was more potent than she thought, because Max took a step back. "You know, you have no right to tell me what I can and can't do. If I want to strip and dance naked at your reception, I can. And besides, I'm not too skinny. Okay, a little bit on the thin side, but it's still extremely rude to point that out, Maxwell."

"Max." Anna's voice was disapproving. She stepped beside Cynthia and put her arm around her shoulders. "Tell me you didn't tell Cynthia she was too skinny."

He pursed his lips. Cynthia knew he was annoyed, because he always did that when he was annoyed. It was odd, knowing the groom as well as she did. This was the first wedding she'd been to where she'd slept with the groom. She giggled and covered her mouth with her hand. But she couldn't stop the laugh that rose, and it came out as a snort.

She tried to regain her composure, but now he was frowning at both of them. Anna leaned closer. "What are you laughing at?"

Knowing Anna would completely appreciate her thoughts, she said, in what she thought was a whisper, "I was just thinking that this is the first wedding I've attended where I've seen the groom naked."

Anna's mouth opened and closed, reminding Cynthia of the large-mouthed bass her father had mounted in his den. Cynthia had the most fabulous feeling that this might be the first time anyone had seen Anna without a comeback.

Then Anna burst out laughing. "Oh my God, there is hope for you yet." She herded Cynthia around some tables. "Come on, sister, we need to powder our noses."

"I don't know about that, but I really have to pee."

For some reason Anna started laughing again, but had herself under control by the time they entered the bathroom. Both women took care of business, then washed their hands.

Anna was smiling. For as long as Cynthia had known her, Anna had always been big in spirit, always happy, always wanting to laugh. Cynthia knew without a doubt, Anna laughed more than Cynthia ever had. She sighed, realizing she was coming off the high of the champagne.

"What's the matter, Cynthia?"

"Nothing." But the moment she said it, her eyes filled with tears.

"Oh, sweetie, I'm sorry. I didn't think you would get depressed today. I thought you were over everything—"

"Oh, no, I'm not really depressed, it's just...I had a scene with Father before I left to come here."

Anna took her by the shoulders and turned Cynthia to face her. "What happened?"

Cynthia smiled at the worry in her friend's voice. And that was how she viewed Anna. A year ago, who would have thought they'd become such good friends?

"He didn't want me coming."

Anna snorted. "That goes without saying. Your brother isn't in town, is he?"

"No." *Thank God.* "It wasn't fun. Father wasn't happy."

She pulled away from Anna. Not because she didn't need the comfort, but because she wasn't good at accepting it. It was hard talking about family business. A Myers did not discuss personal problems with anyone. She had heeded that mantra for years. If she had been able to discuss her feelings with Max, they could have saved themselves a heap of trouble and never gotten engaged.

"What did he threaten you with?"

Studying her friend, Cynthia wondered how much Anna could see beneath Cynthia's artificial surface. More than anyone ever had probably. Anna's clear gaze was tinged with understanding.

"Nothing big." Cynthia fingered the edge of her blouse. "He just kicked me out of the house."

There was a beat of silence. "What will you do?"

She hadn't really thought about it. With everything that had been going on, Cynthia had done her best to ignore the gnawing in her gut. Champagne on an empty stomach, especially with her ulcer, was not the best thing. Add the worry of being homeless, and she didn't even want to think of the doctor bills.

"Not sure. I do have a trust from my grandmother on my mother's side of the family. But, then, I have to find a place to live... Oh, and furniture."

She turned away and busied herself with rewashing her hands. She knew it wasn't her fault, but that didn't stop the humiliation. Heat crept up her neck and into her face.

"Tell you what. You can stay at my place. There's a lot of Max's old fuddy-duddy furniture in there, and I haven't rented it yet. You were going to be house-sitting anyway, so why not just rent it?"

For a second, Cynthia concentrated on washing her hands as she tried to work through her emotions. When she finished, she dried them on a paper towel and looked at Anna. The fact that she had accepted Cynthia, had forgiven her, still amazed Cynthia. Anna treated her better than Cynthia's own family when she truly didn't deserve it. A lump rose in her throat and she swallowed. This...it went beyond letting bygones be bygones.

"Really?" Her voice cracked, embarrassing her.

"Really. Now, let's go round up our men and have some fun. I have plans for Max, and I'm ready to leave."

Cynthia laughed as she tried to put her face back to rights. "I have no man."

"Honey, you may not think so, but Chris Dupree is definitely interested in you."

That gave her an unexpected thrill, but the sensible Cynthia squashed it. No reason to get hot and bothered over a man who was too much for her to handle.

"No."

Anna smiled smugly. "Yes, he is. He could barely take his eyes off you."

"Even if he did, I couldn't handle a man like Chris Dupree. The man is a walking wet dream."

As soon as she said it, her face flushed.

"I must say, that sounds like something *I* would say. I like it. And, although I'll deny it if you tell Max, I agree. Now, why not go take advantage of him?"

"Anna, I couldn't do that."

Anna studied her for a moment. "It isn't because he's black, is it?"

"Oh no. It isn't that. Although I can imagine what my family would say about it."

"Then what is it?"

"Other than Max, there has only been one other guy, and I didn't like it with him, either."

Anna's eyes widened. "You didn't like sex with Max?"

"I don't like sex, period." She shrugged with the familiar feeling of rejection and failure. "It has to be something with me."

Anna crossed her arms beneath her breasts and frowned. "You know, maybe it has to do with the men."

"Oh, come on. First of all, you seem pretty happy with Max." Anna smiled at that. "But I wasn't. And the first one, Brett Simmons—well, he let me know when we broke up that I was a cold fish."

"What I meant was that maybe because these were men

your father picked out for you, you weren't attracted to them. Maybe you need someone your father would disapprove of."

"But I don't know anyone like that."

Anna opened the door and led them out of the bathroom. At the end of the hallway, both Chris and Max stood waiting for them. Max frowned. Chris's mouth curled into a small smile, and Cynthia's heart flip-flopped.

Anna leaned closer. "There's someone who could really show you a good time, and I would say he's someone your father would not suggest you date."

"He lives in Honolulu."

"Even better—a one-night stand."

Cynthia tried to disapprove, but something about the idea excited her. She had never been a one-night-stand kind of woman. It just wasn't done. As she studied Chris, his gaze slid down her body and back up again. Heat flared from her stomach and spread to her sex. She shifted her legs, trying to get rid of all the tingles. It just made it worse. Her damp panties rubbed against her sensitized skin. Her knees went weak.

Lordy.

Anna nudged her in the ribs. "Come on, Cynthia. How often do you get a chance like this?"

"I need a few drinks."

"Tell you what," Anna said as she pulled Cynthia along with her. "Chris needs a ride back to the hotel. Take him, along with a couple of bottles of champagne."

Anna released her and seized Max, dragging him off. She heard Max asking questions and Anna telling him to mind his own damn business.

"Anna says you need a ride." When Chris's smile widened, she realized what she'd said. "Back to the hotel."

He nodded. "Are you offering me a ride?"

The way his voice deepened over the word *ride* made her lose her train of thought. The idea of sitting on his lap, riding him... She swallowed.

"If you're interested." Dang, when did her voice go all husky like that? And when did she start using the word *dang?* Lord, she'd drunk too much.

His lips twitched. "You bet."

"Let me pick up a couple of things, and I'll meet you around front."

He nodded again. As she walked away from him, she felt his gaze on her, sending another jolt of arousal into her blood. Her nipples tightened against the fabric of her blouse.

She grabbed a bottle of champagne and her purse, and released what was left of her sanity. For once, Miss Cynthia Myers was going to go with instinct rather than upbringing. As she rounded the corner of the club, she saw Chris leaning against one of the columns. For just a second, she panicked. What the hell was she thinking? This was completely out of character for her. She shouldn't be doing this, or even thinking it. Being homeless, jobless—those things were important. Jumping the bones of the most delicious man she'd ever met was not.

She must have moved, because he noticed her and smiled. A rush of tingles raced all the way to her toes. Pushing those reservations aside, she decided that for once she needed a little fun. Cynthia Myers needed to let loose. And she was sure Chris Dupree was just the man to help her.

Chris watched Cynthia pour the champagne into the paper cup and tried to remember if there was an open-container law in Georgia. When they had first approached her car, he'd taken the keys from her, making sure not to allow her to drive. He'd thought by the time they made it to the hotel, she would be more sober.

She topped off the cup and planted the bottle between her legs. Fortunately for him, she had to pull up her dress to accomplish it. The woman had a set of legs that he'd kill to have wrapped around his waist. His cock twitched at the thought. Gripping the steering wheel tighter, he turned his attention back to the road. He'd be lucky if he didn't pass out from loss of blood.

"You know," she said and paused to hiccup, then leaned in closer as if to whisper. Instead she yelled in his ear. "This is the first time I wasn't the designated driver."

"Really? I'd never have guessed it. You seem like an experienced drinker."

She shot him a look out of the corner of her eye and snorted. "Little do you know, I have only been drunk once before this. And it was an accident."

He couldn't let that comment go by. "An accident?"

"Yes, see. I have this thing for chocolate."

He waited for her to continue while he took the exit for his hotel. When she didn't explain further, he asked, "What does chocolate have to do with liquor?"

She finished off her cup, making many large slurping noises that he was sure would embarrass her later when she remembered. *If* she remembered.

"That's where the alcohol was, silly."

She giggled. Damn, she was cute when she drank. He knew

she would be horrified when she sobered up, but with her hair mussed and a sloppy smile curving her lips, she was irresistible. He wanted to start at her feet and nibble his way up her body. He was going to have to sober her up some way. While he did, he had to keep his hands off her. And considering the "not quite there" boner he was sporting, that was going to be difficult.

He cleared his throat as he tried to think of what they had been talking about. "So, you ate some chocolate and got drunk. When was this?"

"Christmas, my freshman year at Valdosta State before I switched over to the University of Georgia. Lord, I got so drunk, and just off of rum balls. And you know what?"

When she didn't continue, he realized she hadn't meant it to be rhetorical. "What?"

She looked at him, squinting with one eye. She had the look of a drunk trying to figure out if it were just him standing in front of her or a few others had joined him. "I think that's why I lost my virginity. Brett was really cute, and we were going to some dance, and I thought, 'no big deal'." She grunted. "No big deal, for sure. And he blamed me. I mean, I was the virgin. You would think a senior would know what he was about."

As she talked about sex, it was impossible not to think of what it would be like to hear her moan his name. Visions of silken sheets and warm thighs almost overwhelmed his better senses. Hell, he didn't need much help in contemplating that. The woman might dress like a priss, but when she drank, there was a sensuality to her, from the sway of her hips to the way she smiled. Her sexy nature was restrained, making it all the more tempting to unwrap her and watch her explode.

Dangerous, Chris. She was drunk, and he never took advantage of a woman in her condition.

He pulled into the parking lot of his hotel and found a parking space not too far from the entrance. After getting out and rounding the back end of the car, he opened Cynthia's door. He moved fast to catch her as she nearly fell on her ass.

"Well, thank you, kind sir."

He righted her, his hands at her waist. She giggled again. "You know, I've been wondering what it would feel like to have your hands on me."

Arousal did a sharp upward turn, as did his cock. She leaned against him, wiggling her backside. Her skirt was thin, and with her pressing against him the way she was, his excitement soared. His mouth went dry even as he tried to swallow. Sweat broke out on his forehead as he thought about standing behind her, sliding his cock up her tight ass.

Really not good.

He bit back an oath and reached around to close the car door. He pulled her away from him, making sure there was space between their bodies.

Looking down at her, he laughed. Her hair had passed styled about three cups earlier.

"Why don't we have a little coffee before you go home?"

She stepped back, bumped into her car, crossed her arms beneath her breasts and frowned at him. "I don't have a home anymore."

He sighed, knowing this was going to be hard. Cynthia was definitely not his type, but there was something attractive about her disgruntled expression. He knew he was in trouble then. When a woman looking mean at you turned you on, you were in big trouble, or so his father claimed.

"Listen. We'll worry about home later. Let's drink some coffee and see how you're feeling."

33

"No."

At first, he didn't react. Being the oldest of five siblings, he wasn't used to having his orders thwarted. Especially by a woman who stood about half a foot shorter than him, weighed less than a feather and was drunk because her ex-fiancé had gotten married. But, being in the restaurant business, he knew how to handle a drunk. Even one who was screwing with his ability to think with his big brain and not his little one.

"No, you don't want coffee?"

She shook her head. "I'm not going anywhere without my champagne. Anna gave it to me." Her bottom lip curved out in a perfect pout.

Knowing it would be best to placate her, he shooed her aside and opened the door. After grabbing the champagne bottle, he slammed the door shut, took her by the arm and hurried her inside.

"Thank you, Chris."

Her tone had turned patronizing, as if he were a three-year-old who needed to be soothed. A strange mixture of irritation, amusement and lust swept through him. He wouldn't be surprised if she patted his head.

They walked through the lobby to the elevators. His fingers curled slightly at the feel of warm, bare skin beneath them. As the two of them stepped into the elevator, another couple boarded, and she had to move closer to him. Her scent was driving him crazy. Something flowery, like gardenias. He usually hated those kinds of perfumes, but there was a hint of it on her skin, and it suited the woman. The thought of it on his sheets in the morning, as they both lingered in bed, was tempting. Too tempting.

The other couple got off on the second floor, and as soon as they reached the third floor, he took hold of her by the arm and drew her out of the elevator. She stumbled and then giggled at her clumsiness. He didn't slow down, just dragged her down the hall to his room.

Once there, he released her to pull out his keycard. As he dug into his pocket, she stepped behind him and slipped her arm around his waist. He grabbed his key, resisting the urge to give his cock a nice long stroke through his pants. Chris figured he deserved it, especially because he could feel her breasts pressed against his back, her hard nipples through their layers of clothing. Lord knew he was going to be taking care of himself later, because he didn't see any way of relieving the tension she'd built in him, other than finding another woman or jacking off. Her hand slid up his chest, caressing one nipple, then the other, through his shirt. His fingers fumbled on the card, almost dropping it. As he inserted it into the slot, Cynthia's fingers danced back down his torso, past his abdomen.

He cursed because it took him three times to get the key to work. When the door finally opened, her hand was slithering down to his cock. Chris stumbled over the threshold, breaking free of her hold. Not that it had been that demanding. If he were honest with himself, he would have gladly stood there all day. And that made him madder. She was easily threatening his control, something many women had tried and failed.

Turning, he shot her a glare nasty enough to burn the hair off a hog. She leaned against the closed door, trying to reopen the bottle of champagne. When she noticed his narrowed gaze, she laughed.

"Mr. Dupree." Her voice dripped with Southern seduction. "I do believe you're trying to scare me."

The lust that had simmered all evening exploded into a full boil. Damn, she was smiling at him, those dimples in full force. He didn't need this kind of enticement. It'd been a while since he'd had a woman, or even been that attracted to one. Distance was what he required. He rested a hand on each of his hips and tried to look even nastier. She erupted in a fit of giggles, laughing so hard she lost her balance. She fell on the floor, emitting a squeak when she landed.

It took her several moments to compose herself, but when she did, she said between snorts, "Chris, you can stop trying. You're too sweet looking to be mean."

Exasperated, he rummaged through the dresser and the desk until he found the room-service menu. He didn't like the look in her eyes when she said *sweet*, as if she were talking about more than his personality. The thought didn't disturb him as much as the fact that he wanted to break his rule about drunk women. That, or drink a bottle of Jack Daniels to catch up with her. After ordering coffee, he removed his tie and drew in a cleansing breath. It dawned on him that the room had grown suspiciously quiet. Turning, he checked the floor to see if Cynthia had passed out and panicked when he didn't see her.

Then he noticed the bathroom light on and walked to see what she was up to. Lord only knew, with the amount of alcohol she had swimming in her blood. He found her sitting on the edge of the bathtub, drinking yet another glass of champagne.

He leaned against the doorjamb, watching as she precariously balanced herself and tried to drink. She had lost her jacket, as well as her shoes, somewhere along the way. "You're going to feel like hell tomorrow."

She stared at him, one eye closed tightly. "Well, I don't now."

He laughed, and she smiled, her dimples winking at him.

"Chris?" She lowered her head, but he could tell she was looking up at him through her lashes. The action dripped of coyness, something he usually disdained. But there was an air of innocence to it, as if she didn't realize what she was doing. Again, not his style, but everything about this woman affected him. That disturbed him more than anything else.

"Cynthia?" Even to his own ears, his voice had grown huskier.

She paused, her tongue darting out, gliding along her bottom lip. He bit back the groan that rose in his throat.

Her next question demolished what little restraint Chris had left. "Do you think you'd mind if I licked you up one side and down the other?"

Chapter Three

The silence in the bathroom would normally have had Cynthia moving to fill the uncomfortable gap. Long pauses, tension simmering, her family lived like that. No harsh words were spoken, but silent loathing had been her father's brutal weapon. She'd mastered the skill to cover her insecurities and to banish too many of her childhood memories.

Unfortunately, since she'd met Chris, her usual social skills had fallen by the wayside. From the moment Max first introduced them, she'd been acting like the worst idiot. So, she figured propositioning him was the cherry on top of the sundae.

As he stood there, his face without expression, she realized she may have shocked him. Cynthia Myers was not the type of woman who offered to lick men's bodies, especially those of men she had just met. Something else was driving her on. Something she wanted to feel, something she wanted to do with him. To him.

It was shocking, to say the least. With only two lovers in her past, she'd never lusted after them like this. It was as if someone had lit a match to her soul. All she understood was that it was important she make this work. Desperation clawed at her, pushed her to the edge. Odd, as she'd never had these yearnings before. She'd sort out why later, but now she wanted Chris.

"You've had too much to drink," Chris said.

She glanced up at him, saw the hunger smoldering in his eyes. He wanted her. It baffled her, but he did, and she didn't care why or for how long. Even with need etched in his face, burning in his gaze, he was frowning at her. *Great. I finally decide to throw caution to the wind, and I pick a six-foot dream of a man with a conscience.*

"I haven't had too much to drink." As soon as the words were out of her mouth, she wobbled on the ledge of the bathtub, losing her balance and almost falling backward. Chris stepped forward and grabbed her, pulling her up and saving her from the fall, but spilling champagne on both of them.

She ended up against him, their wet clothes sticking to their skin, making it very easy to feel the contours of his sculpted muscles. Sighing in appreciation, she splayed her free hand against his chest. Her nipples pebbled beneath the damp fabric of her blouse. His breathing deepened. As she slid her hand up over his pecs, she felt his heart beating, fast and hard. She shifted her feet to stand in front of him, her stomach brushing his groin. She stilled, marveling at the rigid shaft pulsing against her. He groaned when she increased the pressure.

"Cynthia, you're pushing me too far."

She laughed with little humor. "I don't think so, Chris."

He stepped away from her, breaking contact. A rush of coolness swept over her skin, into her blood.

"I'm serious. You're a beautiful woman, and you've had too much to drink, especially on a day you saw your ex get married."

Irritation knotted the muscles in her belly because, once again, a man was telling her what she needed. She couldn't win. Jesus, all she wanted was a night of anonymous sex with a man who interested her far more than was good for her.

She settled her hands on her hips and glared at him. "Listen, the only thing I felt today was happiness for Anna and Max."

"Please, even if you are happy for them, it had to hurt a little."

The pity and understanding she heard in his voice, saw in his eyes, embarrassed her. And increased her agitation.

"Listen, I understand." She grabbed her jacket and brushed past him, intent on finding her car keys and going to Anna's. Her body still tingled with arousal, and her mind still spun from champagne, but she would not stay there and be humiliated. She stopped to shove her arms into the sleeves of her jacket. "Figures the one time I decide to do something like this, I get a jackass with morals. I can't even pick men who are amoral. I have to pick a bloody saint."

A sharp knock at the door stopped her tirade. Chris, who had followed her, answered the door without commenting. He stepped aside and allowed the waiter to bring in the tray. After the young man set it on the table in front of the window, he handed Chris the bill, which he signed. After thanking him, Chris closed the door and turned to face her.

"You were saying?"

She growled, which should have shocked her—a Myers never growled. But what shocked her more was the pleased look on Chris's face.

"Nothing. Where are my keys?"

His gaze traveled down, and as before, she felt his attention as if his hands were on her skin. She could imagine his fingers trailing along her flesh, gliding over her breasts, his thumbs touching her nipples. Unwillingly, her body reacted. Her pulse jumped, her skin tingled where his gaze had touched and the muscles in her stomach contracted. By the time he met her gaze, she was trying to resist the urge to wiggle to ease the pressure between her legs.

"You shouldn't drive without having something to eat or some coffee, and taking some time to sober up."

She gritted her teeth, trying her best not to yell. Every man she had known in her life tried to tell her what to do. Even someone she'd planned on using for her one sexual thrill was giving her orders. Her whole being throbbed with desire so strong, it surprised her she didn't pass out.

When she finally composed herself, her voice was low and threatening. "I. Said. Where. Are. My. Keys."

He pursed his lips, and dammit, it made her want to kiss him, made her long to feel his mouth move over her skin.

"In my pocket."

She would have to be an idiot not to hear his New Orleans accent growing more pronounced. She could just imagine hearing that rumbled tone in the dark as he whispered in her ear, his breath hot against her flesh.

Not trusting herself to get too close, she held out her hand.

Chris, damn him, shook his head. "Come get them." Challenge threaded his tone.

This was not a good turn of events. "Excuse me?"

He straightened away from the door, but made no move to approach her. Her gaze traveled down his body to his groin. Excitement lanced through her as she saw the state of his desire.

"I said to come and get them."

She worried her bottom lip with her teeth. It wasn't that she didn't want to do it. Her body pulsed with a strange mix of arousal and fear—strange because it was new to her. Most of the time, when confronted with a decision like this, she automatically did what was expected. For a woman brought up in the sterile environment of the Myers house, that would mean not taking him up on the challenge. But now, alone with Chris, she didn't have to do what other people wanted. She could do what *she* wanted.

"It's not a major decision, *Cyn*thia. Just slip your hand in my pocket and take them." His lips curved.

He did that thing with her name again where he emphasized the first syllable. She knew part of it was seduction, part of it was challenge. And part of her thought maybe he was hoping a direct challenge would send her running away. Gathering her courage, she walked to him, stopping within inches of touching him. She tipped her head back, angling her chin in defiance.

Without breaking eye contact—and he did have the most beautiful eyes, dark brown, threaded with sparks of gold—she reached into his right pocket. When she found it empty, she narrowed her eyes. He laughed.

"I never said it was in that pocket."

Oh, so he wants to play games. Of course, men like him loved to play games. It pleased them to control everything. She was sick of it. Sick of being the one who reacted to everything around her, instead of being the one who caused the reactions. And damned if the idea of dragging control away from him didn't turn her on more. Still, she was irritated. Rational thought dissolved as she considered how she'd allowed men to make decisions for her all her life. Men looked at her and saw a fragile flower without a brain, a woman who couldn't stand up for herself. For once, she refused to let him get away with it. He deserved a little punishment. She shifted her hand an inch and stroked his cock...just once. His smile faded, and every muscle tensed. Triumph flashed through her.

Casually, she pulled her hand from his pocket, grazing the top of his penis with her index finger. He sucked in a breath, and she smiled. An emotion grew inside her chest. It wasn't lust, although it did add an edge to that. It was something else that made her feel more confident...powerful.

"So," she said, leaning closer, taking a deep breath. God, he smelled good. His cologne held a hint of musk mixed with the unique scent of Chris himself. It rose from his flesh, enticing her. Her mouth watered just thinking of nibbling his skin. It made her head spin, her blood flame, her pussy drip. She couldn't think of him as anything but a huge sweet she wanted to take a bite out of. "You have the keys in your other pocket?"

She stepped beside him, dragging her fingers across the front of his trousers, lightly caressing him as she passed by his cock. He leaned his head back against the door and closed his eyes. He took a few deep breaths and swallowed, hard.

"Why don't you find out?"

Again, challenge added an edge to his voice. This time, though, she could tell he hoped she would take him up on it. There was a small space between him and the door, and she slid one leg behind him. She leaned into him, allowing her breasts to brush the back of his arm. With the slightest movement, she rubbed against him. His muscles contracted, and she smiled. He was trying his best to control himself. Wanting to push him a little more and see his reaction, she slipped her hand into his left pocket. She inched her fingers down, massaging the skin beneath the lining of the pocket.

Chris shifted restlessly. She paused until he stilled again. Once he did, she continued her exploration, ignoring the fact she knew damn well her keys weren't in this pocket, either. As before, a sense of power enveloped her. The craving that enticed her now held her body hostage. She'd never been one to initiate. Not once, in all the time she'd been with him, had she pleasured Max. Sex was something always done to her. This was different. This sent another jolt of electric current racing through her blood, pulsing with desire. As she moved closer to him, she felt the dampness of her panties, her pussy clenching when she touched his cock again.

God, she couldn't wait to see him without clothes. Through the thin fabric, she traced the length of him to the flared head. He shuddered in reaction.

"You lied, Chris. There are no keys in your pocket." She tried to sound censorious, but yearning threaded her words, thickened her voice. With one last stroke of her finger across the top of his shaft, she pulled her hand out, then stepped away from him. Not daring to look behind her, she walked further into the room, feeling his gaze slip down her back and concentrate on her ass. The idea that she'd captured his attention almost overwhelmed her. She was positive nothing else crowded his mind but the thought of getting her into bed. She'd never had that kind of hold over any other man. Instead of being frightened by it, her desire soared.

"Cynthia." His voice came out as a groan...a plea. She tried not to smile, but it was hard.

Slowly, she turned and found him standing where she had left him. Considering the way his pants were tented, there was no doubt about his attraction to her. But still he tried to resist, and that not only angered her, but excited her as well. Just thinking of bringing him to his knees, metaphorically, was in and of itself arousing.

"What? You want to pretend you're not turned on?" She tsked. "Really, Chris, I felt that cock."

His eyes widened slightly in shock. She'd sure shocked the

hell out of herself.

"You've had too much to drink."

So, he was going to worry about that. "I'm pretty sober right now." Even though her head was spinning, she was sure it had to do with the situation and not the vat of champagne she'd drunk.

"I..."

He trailed off when she slipped off her jacket and tossed it on the chair beside her. She bent over to remove her shoes, knowing the cut of her blouse probably allowed him to see a good portion of her breasts. When she straightened, he was still stuck to the door, his nostrils flaring.

"Chris, come here."

He hesitated a moment, but then approached her. Another shock of power flashed through her. No one ever did what she told them to. Even asking nicely had crappy results. He stopped within inches of her, his scent capturing her again. She'd noticed men's cologne before, but there was something so basic, so primal about Chris's scent. It called to her, slinked under her skin, sank into her soul.

Moving aside, she grabbed his hand and pulled him along behind her. She eased him into sitting on the edge of the bed and stepped between his legs.

He reached for her, and she shook her head. "Put your hands on the bed." He looked to argue until she added, "You touch me now, and I won't do what I want to."

In a flash, he put his palms down on the bed. As she reached for the buttons on his shirt, her fingers trembled. It wasn't fear, because for once this felt right. It might be all the alcohol, and if so, she should just become an alcoholic. She unbuttoned the shirt and pushed aside the edges to reveal an expanse of light brown skin.

Wanting to see his entire chest, she shoved his shirt off his shoulders. She let it fall around his wrists and placed her hands on his chest. The muscles she'd lusted after were better than anything she could dream up. Even feeling them beneath the wet fabric had not prepared her.

She traced the contours of his chest with her fingers. She circled his dark brown nipples, pinching them, pleased when he groaned. There was a smattering of hair—not much, but a line of it trailed down his stomach and disappeared into his pants. He was so hard she could see the outline of his cock beneath his slacks.

Licking her lips, she undid his belt and unfastened his pants. When she unzipped them, she allowed the backs of her fingers to skim along his hardened length. It twitched against her hand. She pushed aside the fabric, revealing his penis. The engorged head was a shade darker than the rest of his cock, a drop of cum wetting the tip. Reaching out with her index finger, she traced down from the top of his cock.

The only sound in the room was his indrawn breath. He moved his legs, lifting his hands slightly. The moment he did, she pulled her hand back and frowned at him. He watched her, his eyes narrowed, his breathing deep.

"Chris, I said to keep your hands on the bed."

She could see his irritation. He clenched his jaw. Fascinated, she watched defiance mixed with excitement lighten his eyes. After a silent battle, he seemed to come to a decision and slapped his hands back down on the bed.

"That's nice."

He growled, but didn't say a word. Oh my, this was fun. Wanting to see how far she could push him, she stepped back a few feet, just out of reach. She grabbed the hem of her shirt and unhurriedly pulled it off. Throwing it behind her, not caring where it landed, she captured his gaze, challenging him. She wondered how long it would take before he would be tempted to dip his gaze to the rest of her body.

Reaching behind her, she unfastened her bra, shivering as the cool air drifted over her body. The room was chilly, but until that instant she had not noticed how hot her skin was. She let the bra fall to the floor. Once her breasts were bare, his gaze dropped to her naked flesh. She'd never been well endowed, but it hadn't really bothered her before tonight. His tongue darted out, licking his lips. Her imagination didn't have to work hard to conjure an image of his tongue gliding along her skin. Cynthia was sure he would be a genius at driving her crazy with it.

Her nipples tightened almost painfully. Oh Lord. It took every bit of control not to touch them. It would give her some relief, she knew, but she really longed to have his hands on them, his fingers caressing her.

She unzipped her skirt and let it drift to the floor. She stepped out of it, kicked it to the side and smiled at Chris. He didn't even notice. His gaze was fastened on the tiny panties she was wearing. Those, and the pale thigh-high stockings. Both were the only indulgence she had given herself. The pink thong barely covered the important parts. Anna had convinced her to buy the lacy confection when they'd gone shopping and had insisted the thigh-high stockings were essential. Cynthia owed Anna a world of thanks. If the look in Chris's eyes was anything to go by, every penny had been worth it.

She was only a few feet from him, but when she approached him, she walked leisurely. His fingers curled into the bedspread. Excitement lanced through her. Stepping between his legs again, she smiled down at him. He really was adorable.

"You shouldn't be doing this, Cynthia."

The muscle in his jaw jumped as he clenched his teeth. She understood this was his last chance to clear his conscience. The saint was doing battle with the sinner inside.

She shook her head. "Chris, normally I would agree. I'm not a one-night-stand kind of girl." He opened his mouth, and the expression on his face told her he was ready to argue with her. She stopped any further comment by lightly touching her fingers to his mouth. His breath warmed her skin. "No. I want no promises. After tonight, I doubt we'll see each other again."

The need to disagree glittered in his eyes, but he nodded. Something told her he would argue, given half the chance. He was a stubborn man, but for once in her life, she was going to be more stubborn.

"Now, take off your shirt."

He complied, his muscles flexing enticingly as he slid the shirt from around his wrists. Cynthia's heart smacked against her chest. Damn, the man was built. Max had been in good shape, built like a linebacker, with broad shoulders. Just as tall and muscled as Max, Chris resembled a swimmer. He was sinewy, his muscles leaner, more sculpted. She curled her fingers into her palms, trying not to reach out, grab him and take full advantage of that erection he sported for her.

Even just thinking it made her face burn. Again, Anna was to blame. She said exactly what she was thinking. Now she had Cynthia thinking it, but thankfully not saying it out loud. Yet.

When Chris freed his wrists, panic swelled. Old doubts plagued her as she contemplated her next move. What the hell was she doing? Ordering a man around like she was in charge. She didn't even know if she would ever enjoy sex, let alone be able to tell a man what to do to make her happy.

"Cynthia?"

His tone gentle, his warm look told her he'd seen her alarm.

In the face of her weakness, there were no derogatory accusations or condescending remarks. Instead, he offered understanding, just by saying her name.

Arousal now mixed with something more dangerous. *Tenderness.* It unfurled and wrapped her in warmth. She couldn't get attached to him. He was leaving. But the show of understanding, of acceptance she'd never received from anyone, helped shake away any second thoughts she had. It might just be one night, but it was hers to enjoy.

She took his face into her hands and bent her head, giving in to the need that had been clawing at her since she'd first seen him. Lightly, she brushed her lips against his. Satisfaction poured through her as pleasure filled his eyes. Once, twice, three times, she moved her mouth against his. His eyes drifted shut as she pressed harder, his lips opening, allowing her tongue to steal inside.

Lordy. He tasted better than she'd hoped. Soon, she lost control of the kiss as he began to match her, tangling his tongue with hers. Her hands roamed to his hair, then to the back of his head, trying to somehow get close enough to devour him. Nothing in her life had been this delicious, this wonderful. Cynthia broke the kiss, pulling slightly away from him. Both of them were breathing heavily. She swallowed, gathering up her courage for her next demand. It wasn't easy to say the words aloud. This little game had her aroused for the first time in the presence of a man, and there was no way she could stop now. She had to discover if it was real.

"Take off my panties."

Chapter Four

Chris paused for a second as he gathered his control. He didn't want to slide those cotton-candy panties down. He wanted to rip them off, throw her on the bed and sink his cock into her pussy. She would no doubt be tighter than a fist, her muscles clamping down on his shaft. And smelling her, knowing she was wet just from what little foreplay they'd engaged in, wasn't any easier. But he restrained himself. This wasn't about him, about his pleasures. Watching Cynthia gain confidence with her play of domination was more arousing than anything he'd ever observed. Through her pleasure, he would gain his own.

As he reached out, his fingers trembled. For good reason. He was worried with just one touch he would lose it. The woman had him so close to coming. He would bet she didn't even realize the extent of her power over him. Slipping his thumbs beneath the lacy ridge of her panties, he brushed his fingers against her bare ass. Jesus Christ, she was wearing a thong. He'd have loved to see her in it from behind. She was a small woman. The skirt had outlined her curves, showing off her world-class ass. He almost passed out at the memory of it rubbing against his cock. Swallowing, he pulled himself together and gently tugged on the panties. As he moved them down her legs, he skimmed his fingers against her thigh-highs. By the time he arrived at her ankles, his whole body fairly vibrated with need. His dick throbbed, his balls ached, and his brain was no longer functioning. All the blood in his big head had rushed downward.

Daintily—because Cynthia did everything that way, even when she was ordering him about—she stepped out of the panties. When he straightened, the thatch of curly blonde hair, a shade darker than that on her head, caught his attention. Neatly trimmed, the curls were wet with her passion, the musky scent filling his senses. Damn, she smelled good.

"Chris."

He loved the way she said his name. Long, lazy, Southern. It wound its way down his spine, sent his heartbeat out of control. He looked up and smiled, hoping to placate her. She was frowning at him, that wrinkle appearing between her eyebrows. In the few short hours he'd known her, Chris had found himself observing small mannerisms most people probably overlooked. He noticed things about women all the time, but Cynthia didn't seem to be able to hide her emotions from him. He had a feeling she'd masked them for years. It gave him satisfaction to know she couldn't do that with him. Whether it was the alcohol, or him, it didn't matter. All he cared about was that he was the lucky bastard she had chosen for her wild night of sex.

"Yes, Cynthia?"

She drew in a deep breath and swallowed. Even in the dim light he could see her pulse beat a rapid tattoo in her throat. For all her bravado, this was hard for her. The power was intoxicating. Personal experience taught him the unbelievable thrill of domination. But for someone like Cynthia, someone who had no experience in this sort of thing, it could be just as frightening.

"You're wearing too many clothes." The words came out in

a whispered rush, as if she were afraid of saying what she desired. Chris was sure he could teach her that there was nothing wrong with what she wanted.

He couldn't stop the tiny smile that statement caused. "And what would you have me do about it?"

She stepped back, the outsides of her thighs brushing his. His skin already burned with the need to be caressed by her hands, by her mouth. The fabric of his pants rubbed against his inner thighs and his balls, increasing his arousal. *Jesus.* Another jolt of heat rushed through him. A slight touch and he was ready to explode. He resisted the urge to give his cock a stroke because he wasn't sure he wouldn't blow his load with that one pump.

"Stand up." This time her voice was more forceful, more confident. And damn if there wasn't another burst of lust warming his blood at that sound.

He complied, his pants undone, hanging on his hips. She walked around him, gently urging him to step away from the bed. The bedsprings squeaked as she sat down.

"You can turn around."

He did, knowing the rules of the game even if she didn't. When he saw her reclining on the bed, one arm over her head, those pretty pink nipples hard and pointing right at him, it was hard not to say *fuck the game* and jump her right then and there. She must have seen something in his face because when he met her gaze, her eyes widened. He curled his fingers into his palms.

Her gaze slipped down his body, her breath hitching when she reached his groin. She licked her lips, and his dick twitched, another drop of cum rising to wet the head.

She cleared her throat. "Now, take off your pants." He grabbed the waistband, but she stopped him with her next comment. "And do it slowly."

The gritty determination in her voice resembled a command rather than a request. Her excitement, and the strength he felt growing within her, awakened something he thought dead. This went beyond lust or desire. She was lying there on the bed, wearing nothing but a pair of thigh-highs, tossing commands at him.

As she'd ordered, he slid his pants down. Once he'd tossed them to the side, along with his socks, he straightened. Her pink tongue swept over her plump lips again, leaving behind a glaze of wetness. She was going to drive him crazy with that tongue. He could imagine it gliding down his chest, past his stomach, to his—

"Turn around."

Again, he was struck by the command in her voice. She was gaining confidence and driving him out of his mind in the process. He did as instructed. When he turned so that he faced away from the bed, he stopped moving. She shifted her weight and the bed creaked. His breath caught in his throat as she approached him. Chris didn't need sound to tell him she was near. Her feminine musk mixed with her perfume was strong enough for him to smell, but there was also something else, something electric in him when she drew closer. As if Cynthia flipped a switch within him.

"Back up a bit."

The instant his legs touched the bed, her hands were on him. At first, they glided down his back. When they reached his ass, she hesitated, then continued on. Her breathing deepened as her fingers whispered across his skin.

"Oh my." The breathless sigh sent a rush of warmth that sank beneath his flesh. She continued to murmur her approval as she bent forward. Her hair brushed against him as she touched her lips to the fullest part of one ass cheek. It was an open-mouthed caress, her tongue swiping along his skin, her teeth following. He shuddered. She moved from one cheek to the other, her hand replacing her tongue as she went along.

Slowly, she worked her way up his back. As her mouth slid against his flesh, the words she'd said earlier echoed in his mind. Her tongue darted out before each kiss.

He'd done a lot in the bedroom, tried just about every scenario his mind or any of his partners' could conjure up, but never in his life had he felt this. It was as if she were savoring him, tasting him like a forbidden treat. Her hands snaked around his waist and slipped up to his chest as she pressed her body against his back. Murmuring incoherently beneath her breath, she nipped his earlobe, then licked. The action caused him to curl his toes into the carpet. By the time she shifted to the other ear, her fingers were caressing his nipples, pinching them slightly. His knees went a little weak.

Much to his disappointment, she stopped. She scooted around him and stood, then, completely taking him by surprise, she pushed him. Not being prepared, he lost his balance and fell onto the bed, bouncing once before she pounced on him. She straddled his hips, placed her hands on either side of his head and grinned down at him. Her hair was even more out of control than before, her eyes filled with desire. This wasn't the timid creature he'd met earlier in the day. This was a temptress. And he was going to reap the rewards.

Her hips gyrated, her pussy pressing against his cock. He closed his eyes, trying to ignore her damp heat. Temptation beckoned. Chris knew he was moments from slipping into her sweet sex and finding satisfaction. She sat up, forcing her cunt harder against his dick.

He opened his eyes, and his mouth went dry. She'd crossed

her arms beneath her breasts. There was no way for him to resist. Sitting up, he reversed their positions and fastened his mouth on her breast the moment she was settled. Sweet Jesus, she tasted good. As he transferred his attention to her other breast, her legs shifted restlessly. He grazed his teeth over her nipple. She gasped, then moaned when he did it a second time.

He moved down her body, his own throbbing, begging for release. But Cynthia's pleasure came first. Soft as a rose petal, the skin of her stomach quivered as he dipped his tongue into her navel. When he reached her dripping pussy, he drew in a deep breath. The blonde curls were damp with her need. His mind spun at the sweet musky scent of her arousal.

Looking up at her, he waited for her approval. She pulled herself up to her elbows and nodded. He caught her gaze and leaned forward and licked her slit. Moaning, she allowed her head to fall back, her eyes drifting closed. He placed a hand on each thigh, pushing them wider, and slipped his tongue between her folds. Her taste exploded in his mouth. Sweet, with a hint of sass, just like the woman herself, and he couldn't get enough of her. As he continued to lick her, he thrust one finger into her cunt. Holy Mother of God. Her muscles clamped down on his finger with the grip of a linebacker. He couldn't wait to drive his cock into her pussy.

She moved against his mouth. As her moans grew louder, he felt the tension within her grow, tighten, push to the edge. He knew she was close, so he pressed his thumb on her clit once...twice...

She exploded, her body convulsing with her orgasm. He pulled back, continuing to caress her as she came, but enjoying the sight of her was too much to resist. Her eyes were closed, her hair a tangled halo around her head, her mouth open and moaning his name. The sight was almost as satisfying as if it were his own orgasm. Moments later, she settled, her body going limp. Knowing he would not survive another incident like that, he jumped off the bed, grabbed his wallet and drew out a condom.

In record time, he had it on and returned to the bed. He covered her body with his. Cynthia opened her eyes halfway and smiled at him. His heart flipped and took a dive at the sight of her lips curving with satisfaction, her body loose-limbed from her orgasm.

He bent his head and took her lips in an openmouthed kiss. Cynthia responded immediately, her tongue tangling with his. As he devoured her mouth, he shifted his hands down to her hips, angling them the way he liked. She protested when he pulled away, but he would not be deterred. Taking his cock in one hand, he positioned it at her entrance. As he slid into her pussy, her eyes shut, but not before he witnessed desire rising again. He captured her hips with both hands and pushed further into her warmth. Even though she was dripping with arousal, she was tight as a virgin. Inch by inch, he entered her, allowing her muscles a second or two to adjust. By the time he was in her to the hilt, his body screamed for release. She wrapped her legs around his waist as he began to move.

Chris wanted to take it slow, but as her head thrashed about on the pillow and she moaned his name—begging, demanding that he go faster—he moved to his knees, changing his angle. As he continued to thrust in and out, her moans grew, her body tightened around his, and she came again. Her pussy clasped his cock, drawing it deeper, milking him. Chris thrust hard into her as his balls drew tight. In that one moment, he hurtled over the edge and his body exploded, her name on his lips.

Minutes later, he collapsed on top of her and rolled over, reversing their positions. Their legs tangled together, the scent of their passion filled the air. Cynthia shifted on top of him, trying to get comfortable, and emitted a dainty snore. A smile curved his lips at the satisfaction coursing through him. As he drifted off to sleep, he realized he'd just experienced a tiny bit of Cynthia's sensuality. Once he taught her about the power of control, how to give and how to take, Chris was sure the woman would be unstoppable.

Cynthia awoke in small degrees. She opened her eyes and noticed two things. The dark shadows told her it still wasn't morning. Secondly, the white wallpaper with huge roses signaled she wasn't in her room or Anna's. Still groggy, it took several seconds for her mind to focus. When it did, the memories of the evening came rushing back. The drinking, the kissing, the...

Oh God, she'd practically ordered Chris Dupree into bed. She'd acted like some militant nympho. How was she ever going to face him?

Shifting her legs, she encountered bare skin, a tad bit hairier than her own. She froze. Lordy, she was still in bed with him. Of course she was. Where the hell else would she be? It wasn't like he would get up and leave his own hotel room.

Slowly, trying not to disturb him, she shimmied to the edge of the bed. The moment she reached it, his arm snaked around her waist, pulling her back against him. Excitement mingled with embarrassment at the feel of his hard cock against her rear end.

"Not trying to sneak away, are you?"

His voice was rough with sleep, his accent thick, and dammit, she melted at the sound. He chuckled before she could form an answer. "Of course you were. Scared the hell out of yourself, didn't you?"

He kissed the back of her neck, and she shivered.

"I—I don't normally do things like this."

He rubbed his shaft against her and chuckled again.

Exasperated, she sighed. "Chris, this is a one-time—"

"Now, don't make me prove I'm worth more than one time. I'd think the first time would have done that."

Even as she tried to resist, his arrogance made her smile. From the feel of his erection, he definitely had a reason for it. He began kissing and licking her earlobe, making it difficult to form an argument.

"You live in Hawaii. I live in Georgia. And although I love Hawaii, it would make it one hell of a commute with me living here."

"You've been to Hawaii? Which island?"

"Oahu. My grandmother owned a house close to the North Shore."

"Ahh." And he went back to kissing her. His hand slid to her hip, and he pulled her tighter against him. "What else?"

Her whole body seemed to be an instrument made for him to play. He touched her, and she wanted to perform Beethoven's Fifth. "What?"

"What other argument do you have for us not...enjoying each other again?"

"Ahh...oh. Yes." She sounded all breathless, her body warming as his fingers danced down her abdomen and covered her sex. "We're very different. I mean, I'm sure you are used to being so in tune..." She swallowed as he slipped one finger between her folds. "But I have had problems getting satisfaction..."

He moved his finger, brushing against her clit. If she weren't already so excited, she would be embarrassed by the gush of liquid probably wetting his hand.

"But you had no problem with me." Again, his pride made her smile. He removed his hand from her pussy. She heard the sound of foil ripping and knew he was donning another condom. A moment later, something bigger than his fingers prodded at her entrance. Without thought, she lifted her leg, and he pushed into her.

"Ah, *chéri*, you fit me like a glove." His accent thickened, the sound of it brushing along her nerve endings.

As he pulled out and then thrust back into her, he murmured incoherently in her ear. The tension built, her desire spiraling through her. She pressed back against him, needing more of him, all of him. Her head clouded, her senses filled with him—his scent, the feel of his skin against hers, the sound of his voice teasing her. She tried her best to increase the momentum, but he kept it slow and easy. All the while, he kept talking, telling her just what he wanted to do to her. Part of it was in French, part in English. The pictures he painted with his words pushed her closer to the edge.

She felt herself teetering, but not near enough. She crept closer to fulfillment, but he paused. Reaching around her, he grabbed an extra pillow, laid it on the bed, and rolled both of them on top of it. Positioning her just right, his hands on her hips, he drew himself up to his knees and began driving into her again, pushing deeper than he had been before. She pulled herself up to her elbows and knees, making it easier for him.

Chris kept one hand on her hip, the other sliding around to tease her clit as he continued to thrust heavily into her.

"Ah, *chéri*, that's it. Baby, come for me. Come apart for me."

He pressed her clit, moving his fingers in a circular motion.

The tension that had been building from the minute his hands had touched her coiled in her stomach, then radiated to her sex. One more plunge into her core, and she came, her body splintering into a thousand shimmering pieces. He sustained his rhythm as she convulsed. She started to relax, the last of her orgasm diminishing, as Chris dove harder, deeper, his fingers still on her clit. Without allowing her to recuperate from her first one, he pushed her over into another mind-shattering orgasm. This time, he joined her, shouting her name as his body covered hers.

Time passed as the only sound filling the hotel room was their breathing. He rolled to his side, pulling out of her. She felt the mattress rise as he left. Turning to her side, she watched as he discarded the condom. He returned to bed wearing nothing but a sleepy, satisfied smile. Sliding in beside her, he drew her close, one hand skimming down her back to her rear end. She placed her head on his chest beneath his chin. He grunted in satisfaction and rubbed her rear.

"Now, *chéri*, no more talk of just one time."

She could hear the teasing in his voice, but she didn't smile. She was trying hard not to cry. Blinking away the tears, she reminded herself that this was about tonight, about enjoying the moment. That was all she'd have.

Yearning filled her as she imagined waking up with him, laughing with him, loving... Oh no. She would not fall for that. She didn't know the man, so she wasn't in love. She was in lust, and that fizzled out. Just because she'd had good—no, *great*—sex, didn't mean she was in love. There was a connection—that, she could admit to herself—but it was based on sex. Her life was a mess, and she didn't need more complications. It didn't stop her from wanting it, craving it, though.

Thinking of one of Anna's favorite sayings, Cynthia now

understood exactly what Anna meant when she said it.

This sucked, and not in a good way.

Chapter Five

Chris watched Cynthia dress, a mixture of immense satisfaction and irritation running through him. The night they'd shared had only whetted his appetite for her. He wanted to show her just what she needed in bed, show her the power of domination. What she'd started hadn't been full domination, but the glimpses he'd seen the night before told him she wanted—hungered—to learn her full powers.

Someone with Cynthia's background would require several months to work through the emotions her new role would bring out. All he'd had was a night. Chris knew without a doubt she would enjoy that role and, in the end, be his perfect mate when she submitted to him. She didn't realize what they had together. That, paired with the fact she was running away at the light of day, caused the irritation.

"I don't have to leave until late tonight. Why don't you spend the day in bed with me?"

She sighed as she zipped her skirt. "I told you. Anna and Max are leaving today. I need to get to her house. I'm also responsible for making sure her shop runs smoothly. If there are any problems, I'm the one who has to bother her. I don't want that to happen."

He mulled that over as she pulled her shirt over her head and then looked around for her shoes. As she bent over, the memory of taking her from behind flashed before him. He'd found her wild, crazy...perfect. He couldn't wait to introduce her to anal play. He was sure she'd love it. Shaking his head to push away the thoughts of slipping into her tight little ass, he brought himself back to his argument.

"You could go there, get everything straight and come back." It surprised him how close he was to pleading with her to stay. He'd never even contemplated begging with any other woman, but with Cynthia, he didn't want to lose their connection. Glancing at the clock, seeing it was just after six thirty, he formulated another plan. Since her back was turned to him, he slid from bed and snuck up behind her. "Anna and Max aren't leaving until tonight."

She jumped when he spoke, then looked over her shoulder at him. "Chris, I should have left last night."

"You're embarrassed to be seen with me." He said the words, worried they might be true. He didn't think Cynthia was prejudiced, but he was in South Georgia, the heart of Dixie. It was different from Honolulu. Her family came from old Southern money, the kind that didn't like to mingle with people of color—unless they were being served by them. But besides the color of Cynthia's skin, there was the added problem of her background. She'd been taught to be ashamed of her sexuality. Even as she frowned at him, he slipped his arms around her waist and pulled her to him.

She settled against his chest. Her golden hair contrasted against his dark skin. He drew in a deep breath. The hint of her flowery perfume lingered beneath the scent of sex coating her skin.

"You know I'm not embarrassed to be seen with you. In fact, I would probably gain points for the gossip it would cause."

He heard the smile in her voice and responded in kind.

She shook her head. "It isn't being seen with you that would bother me. It is everyone knowing...well, knowing."

Resting his chin on top of her head, he gently rocked her. "What does that matter? Everyone knew about you and Max."

The sigh she released was filled with irritation. "Yes, they did. But, you see, I was marrying Max. A Myers doesn't have one-night stands."

He heard the scorn in her voice. He hoped it was more for what she'd had to endure than what had occurred between them. Glancing over his shoulder, he located a chair just a few steps back.

"Tell you what," he said as he walked both of them to the chair. "Why don't we have breakfast, and then you can go?"

When he reached the chair, he sat, pulling her down with him. She wiggled and crossed her arms beneath her breasts. Breasts he wanted to touch, lick, taste. Since he was nude, he knew she felt his erection. She stilled, looking down at him, her eyes simmering with passion.

"Chris." She was trying to sound like she disapproved. It wasn't working. Mainly because he could see the pulse in her neck jump and hear her breathing increase. "You would think..."

She closed her eyes as he grabbed hold of her hips and ground against her. "Think what?" He nipped at her earlobe.

She drew in a shuddering breath. "Chris..."

This time, there was such yearning in her voice it made him want to shout with triumph. She needed him like he needed her and playing fair was off the table. Knowing how sensitive her breasts were, he slid one hand up under her blouse and beneath the fabric of her bra. A few strokes of his thumb was all it took. Her nipple pebbled, and she moaned.

"Come on, *chéri*. Once more."

And even though he said it, he silently acknowledged once would never be enough. He'd never felt this connection with a woman, the need to bring her into her own, to teach her the things that would make her complete. He moved his hand to caress her other breast, and she relaxed against him.

"This is our one chance." He didn't believe that. He would figure out some way to make it work, even thousands of miles apart. "Why would we not enjoy ourselves?"

She shuddered, her rear end wiggling over his erection. As the blood rushed from his brain, he had to beat back the caveman who said to throw her down and show her just how good they were together.

He slid his hand beneath her skirt. As he skimmed one finger along her slit, he pinched her nipple with the fingers of his other hand. Her gasp was filled with surprise and arousal.

"Chris..."

Her sex was so damp her panties soaked with her passion. She moved with him, her body taking over even if she still harbored doubts.

"That's it, baby. So wet."

In one abrupt motion, she pulled away from him and off his lap. He opened his mouth to argue with her, but she shook her head. She settled her hands on her hips, her breath coming out in gasps. Licking his lips, he noticed her nipples pushing against the fabric of her shirt.

"You know, you like to tell people what to do. But I'm not sure I want that."

Again, his mouth opened in protest, but she touched her index finger to the tip of his cock, spreading around the beads of moisture that had bubbled up. Catching his gaze, she lifted her hand to her mouth, licking her fingers. A simple act, but it was probably one of the most erotic things he'd witnessed in his life. She put her finger between her lips, sucking the rest of the liquid off.

When she finished, she slid her finger out and smiled. "I was right, Mr. Dupree. You are delicious." Her voice dripped with seduction, arousal, her Southern accent deepening, turning him inside out. He moved to stand, but she stepped forward and placed her hand on his shoulder.

"Uh, uh, uh. Mr. Dupree, I think we are having problems communicating here." She trailed her fingers over his chest as she walked around the chair. Once she was behind him, she settled her hands on his shoulders, rubbing his tense muscles. "I think for once I should be the one to decide about this. True, you played along with me yesterday, but I don't know if you suffered enough."

He wanted to tell her that he had not been playing along. That he understood her need to dominate. She stole any rational thought as she moved her hands to his head, massaging his scalp. Chris closed his eyes and leaned his head back to rest on her breasts.

"You know, I have a feeling you enjoyed yourself last night."

He chuckled. "How did you guess?"

She ignored that comment. "But you know what? I don't think you ever told me what you like."

Her hands skimmed down his face, past his chest and stomach, to his cock. He was held mesmerized watching her elegant, ivory hands contrasting against his darker skin as they moved down his body. Leaning against his shoulder, she draped her body over his and took hold of him at the base.

"It was all about making me happy, which is good. I don't know if anyone ever thought about that before. But you know what would make me happy?" She nipped at his ear, then licked it.

"What?"

She stroked him again, allowing her thumb to pass over the head. "I want to drive you crazy."

"You're doing a good job of it right now, Cynthia."

She pumped him a few times. Tension gathered along his nerve endings, his body coiling, reaching for the pinnacle. His balls were so tight, he was amazed he had held on this long.

"Not good enough, in my opinion."

Once more she stroked him, teasing him with the release he needed, then she was gone and walking around the chair again. His body was pulsing, clamoring to reach fulfillment, and she left him. He opened his eyes and found her in front of him. Without a word, she dropped to her knees. She placed a hand on each of his legs and leaned forward. Touching her tongue to the base of his cock, she licked up one side, swiped over the top, and down the other side.

"Sweet. You taste so sweet." He didn't miss the excitement in her voice. She made him sound like a tasty confection, one she would relish, lick by lick, until she had completely devoured it.

She wrapped one hand around the base, took him into her mouth. She couldn't take his entire length, but she did her damnedest. Closing her eyes, she set to work, sucking, kissing, licking him, driving him out of his ever-loving mind. Again, the tension mounted. He curled his toes, trying to hold off. Just as he felt he might not be able to stop his orgasm, she pulled away.

He looked down and almost came at the sight of her tongue darting out over her swollen lips.

"Hmmm." That was all she said before she leaned forward to lick and suck his balls. Jesus. He'd created a monster.

Before he was satisfied, she was moving away again. She stood, wiggled out of her skirt, tugged off her shirt and bra and unhurriedly removed her panties. Grabbing the one condom left, she tore it open, pulled it out and approached him.

"Now," she said as she bent over to put it on. "You be a good boy, and I'll be nice."

The teasing in her voice was new, but there was also another element. Steel laced her words, telling him that at this point she was in control. Once the condom was on, she stepped back and paused. Chris realized she was waiting for him to agree. Not able to form words—kind of hard with all the blood drained from his head—he nodded.

She smiled at him as if he owned the world, and at that moment, he thought he did. Approaching him, she straddled his hips and slid down his cock. Her ultra-tight pussy gripped him, caressing his dick with each movement.

When she finally slid all the way down, she leisurely began to rise. Deliberately, he was sure, she moved slowly, riding him at a pace guaranteed to drive him insane. Irritated, frustrated and out of patience, he grabbed hold of her hips, wanting to urge her to move faster. In less than a second, she captured his wrists and tugged them behind his head.

Looking down at him with eyes filled with arousal, she shook her head. "No, Chris." Even though her voice was breathless, she projected the aura of someone in charge. Another jolt of lust lanced through him, increasing his hunger, pushing him on. There was nothing in this world as sexy as a Domme realizing her power.

She began to increase her speed. He could tell she was close. Her muscles tightened around his shaft, pulling him deeper. Within moments, she was out of control, slamming down on him hard. She released his hands to cup his face as her mouth settled on his in a wet, openmouthed kiss.

Her pussy contracted on his cock. She devoured his mouth, her moans coming out muffled. When she tore her lips away, she leaned her head back, closing her eyes. "Now, Chris, baby, come with me now."

That plea pushed him over the edge, and as she shuddered with her release, he followed, the tension in his body bursting free as he came.

Long minutes passed until he shook himself out of his stupor. Cynthia was draped over him, his cock still inside of her, her breath shuddering across his skin. He drew her tighter against him, and she snuggled, like a kitten in need of attention. With what little strength he had left, he lifted both of them out of the chair, eased out of Cynthia and laid her on the mattress. After discarding the condom, he stood beside the bed and watched her sleep. It was hard to believe this was the same woman who had blushed just the day before when she held his hand.

Warmth spread through his chest, his heart almost dropping to his stomach when he realized that she could really get to him. He'd given up hope of finding someone who might be comfortable with his role as a switch. Women didn't always accept a man who didn't want to control every time in bed. Especially in the lifestyle. They expected you to pick one side or the other. Be dominant or submissive. But in Cynthia, he thought he might have found a woman who could accept him and his desires.

He just didn't expect to need her so much. Shaking his head, he climbed into bed with her and pulled her up next to him. Contentment filled the sigh she released as she rubbed her head against the underside of his jaw. As his *maman* had always said, he wouldn't borrow trouble. He would take one day at a time.

☯

Cynthia removed one tray of chocolate chip cookies, placed it on top of the stove and put another prepared tray inside the oven. When she'd left Chris just a couple of hours earlier, she hadn't expected to feel this...lonely. She'd only met the man the day before, and now it felt like she had lost a part of herself. Silly, she knew, and a bit juvenile, but she couldn't help it. And even if she could, she didn't want to.

She'd discovered a new part of herself with Chris. *Bold* wasn't a word people used to describe her. Hell, most people didn't even notice her when she was standing right next to them. But last night, and especially that morning, she'd shocked the heck out of herself. Not once in her past had she initiated sex, let alone done the things she'd done to Chris. She couldn't really help it. There was a way about Chris, something in the way he looked at her, treated her, that made her want to take chances. And when she did, the surge of power gained from it was almost as frightening as it was invigorating.

She shook away those reflections and continued on with her task. As she removed the cookies to the rack to cool, she heard the sound of a car pulling into the driveway. She cringed, considering what Max had thought of her going off with Chris the night before. Max would always be the big brother she wished she'd had, rather than the one she did have. Her feelings of embarrassment had nothing to do with their past romantic relationship. There had been little romance and lots of business dealings tied to their proposed marriage. She just didn't want to disappoint him.

As usual, Anna burst into her house. Anna never did anything by half measures, from all her curly hair that she couldn't control, to the way she dressed, to the way she behaved. Cynthia had envied her from the time they'd met in high school.

"Cynthia!" Anna pulled her into an embrace, and for the first time, Cynthia truly returned the hug. Physical contact wasn't something she was accustomed to. Her family disdained it. Anna let go and smiled at her. "Gonna tell me what happened last night?"

Anna glanced around the kitchen, which was still a mess from Cynthia's frenzy of baking. Measuring cups and mixing bowls littered the countertops along with a smattering of flour.

"What the hell is all this?"

"I...I tend to bake when I need to think."

Max joined them. Without an invitation or even a word to either one of them, he helped himself to a handful of cookies.

"Bake?" Anna asked, grabbing a cookie out of Max's hand. She popped it into her mouth and hummed, closing her eyes. After swallowing, she reopened her eyes. "This is not simply baking. You used macadamia nuts, but these cookies are richer than the ones I make."

Cynthia smiled. "I raided your liquor cabinet. Just a little Kahlua before you add the nuts and chips. Works well with cakes, also."

"It gives them more of a decadent taste. I mean, the chocolate melts, but the cookie itself seems to dissolve the moment it touches your tongue," Anna said, seizing another cookie Max had just picked up.

He frowned at her and smiled at Cynthia. "You know, if I'd

known you could bake like this, I might have tried harder to hold onto you."

Anna laughed even as she punched his arm and turned her attention to Cynthia. "Where did you learn to bake like this?"

Cynthia didn't want to admit her best friend growing up had been the family cook. It was embarrassing how starved she'd been for anyone to notice her that she'd spent days in the kitchen learning to bake.

Instead, she shrugged. "I enjoy it. I always have had a knack for baking."

Anna took a bite of her cookie as Max noticed her banana nut muffins. Anna moaned in obvious appreciation.

"You looking for a job?" Anna asked as she snatched a second cookie. Before Cynthia could answer, she faced Max and said, "Don't you think three pancakes, eggs and sausage were enough for breakfast?"

He wiggled his eyebrows at Anna. The gesture reminded Cynthia just how much Anna had loosened Max up. He never would have teased her like that. "I worked up quite an appetite last night."

Anna rolled her eyes and grabbed Cynthia's arm. "We have to have some girl talk."

"But my cookies—"

"You have the timer on, right?"

Cynthia nodded.

Anna looked at her husband. "Max, take the cookies out when the timer goes off."

She tugged Cynthia along, practically dragging her upstairs. When they reached her old room, she pulled Cynthia inside and shut the door behind her.

"You know one thing I've always liked about you, Anna?"

Cynthia asked as she watched Anna open the closet door.

"What?" Anna ducked her head inside, rummaging around on the floor for something.

"You know how to be subtle."

Anna swiveled around so fast she fell on her rear end. She frowned up at Cynthia, then smiled when she realized Cynthia had been joking.

"Can't be subtle with Maxwell. Subtle for him is a two-by-four to the head."

Cynthia laughed and sat on the bed. "What are you looking for?"

"I have this great pair of flip-flops with cherries on them." She began to look around again. "So, you going to tell me, or am I going to have to ask?"

Cynthia sighed. She'd known this was coming and that Anna would expect to gossip. Girl talk wasn't something Cynthia did. She'd had acquaintances, but never any kind of girlfriends she would divulge secrets to. Not that she'd had anything really shocking to talk about before now.

Before Chris Dupree.

"I took Chris to his hotel room."

"A-ha!" Anna stood, her hair hanging in her face. Triumphantly, she held up a pair of red flip-flops with a set of cherries dangling from each thong. She shoved her hair out of her face with the other hand. "I knew they were here. Max went on about how it didn't matter, I could buy more, blah, blah, blah. So, what happened?"

"With Chris?" Cynthia tried to act nonchalant, but she could hear her voice rise.

"Yes, with Chris." Anna groaned. "You didn't actually waste a perfectly good body and do the right thing, did you? Please tell me you did something bad."

Cynthia thought about her seduction, the way they'd made love the last time, him in the chair...

Her face flushed, and Anna laughed. "Ahh, you didn't waste it. Okay, how was it? Tell me it was worth it."

How was it? How did she describe the best sex of her life? She smiled, and Anna hugged her.

"If it was that good, I'm glad I pushed you to do it. Every woman deserves a man who puts that look on her face."

Anna released her. "Now, about that job. When I return, I would like you to start baking for me."

"Anna, really, I have enough money."

Anna threw the shoes on her bed. "Listen, Cynthia, this isn't about money. This is about making some of the most sinful cookies I've ever tasted. Plus, you know that Gerard is leaving after I return, and I'm going to need help. I take it you can do all varieties, and muffins?" Cynthia nodded. "What about biscotti?"

Cynthia grinned, remembering the spring break trip she'd taken to a cooking school. While other students were baking in the Florida sun, she had been learning all kinds of baking techniques. "Yes, several types. Almond is one of my favorites, but I do make a wonderful macadamia nut biscotti. My own recipe."

Anna closed her eyes and sighed in appreciation. When she opened them, Cynthia saw the businesswoman no one messed with. "Okay, you don't have a choice. You *are* working for me."

There was a knock at the door, and before either of them said a word, Max opened it. He was wearing his brotherly frown, and immediately she was worried. Was her father or brother here? Had they called? Tension coiled in her stomach, a sharp pain radiating from the center.

"Chris Dupree is on your phone." He held out her cell phone.

Anna smirked, and he noticed and frowned harder at her. Not wanting any more tension, Cynthia tried to intervene.

"Thanks, Max." She held her hand out, but he pinned her with a glare.

"How did he get your number?" His suspicious tone irritated her. He had no right to question her.

Before she could stop herself, she answered, "I gave it to him when I left his room." He looked somewhat relieved, so she went in for the kill. "This morning."

He opened his mouth, but Anna, thank the good Lord, stopped him by grabbing the phone and handing it to her. "We'll be downstairs."

As soon as the door shut, Cynthia's heart began to beat harder. Her mouth suddenly went dry. Lifting the receiver to her ear, she tried again to sound casual.

"Hello, Chris."

"Hey, *chéri*. How are you doing?"

She shouldn't fall for it, but his lyrical voice melted some of her reserve. "Doing okay. I just left a few hours ago."

He exhaled, a sound so plaintive it made her laugh. "Yes, I know, but, darlin', I'm already missing you."

A little thrill raced down her spine. She'd never had a man say that to her. Even though she knew it was harmless flirting, it didn't stop her heart from doing somersaults.

"Max didn't sound too happy to talk to me."

"Oh, he's just playing big brother. Don't worry about him."

"Hmm, well I don't like him playing anything with you." His

voice hardened just a bit, taking on an edge she hadn't heard before. He grunted, as if trying to control his temper. When he spoke, his voice had softened again. "So, what are your plans today?"

"I told you I was coming over here to Anna's."

"You did that. Now do you want to do something fun?"

She laughed. "Yeah, what do you have in mind?"

There was silence for a second, and she realized he had expected her to fight him on it. Then he said, "How about dinner?"

"You're leaving in a few hours."

"So is that a no?"

"You don't have time. I would feel guilty if you missed your flight."

"You're a hard woman to pin down. I get back to Hawaii late your time, so how about I call you tomorrow?"

She wanted to ignore the excitement that one comment caused, but it was hard. Especially since her body was already reacting to the way his voice flowed through the phone. She shivered. "Chris, you really don't have to do that."

"Ahh, but, *chéri*, I do. More than you know." He paused as if he were contemplating his next words carefully, but simply said, "I'll talk to you later, *Cyn*thia."

After she hung up, she pushed the conversation aside. As she headed back to the kitchen, she decided she wouldn't wait to hear from him. She would only be disappointed if he didn't call. She would not make plans; she would play it by ear.

Stopping midway down, she realized that was something new for her. She plotted everything, planned things down to the smallest detail. Ms. Cynthia Myers didn't just go with the flow. A smile curved her lips, and she practically floated down the stairs. When she reached the first floor, she joined Max and Anna in the kitchen, where he was devouring more cookies.

Both of them looked at her, Anna expectant, Max frowning as he munched away.

"Anna, I'll take you up on that offer of working for you."

Chapter Six

A month after her announcement to Anna, Cynthia smiled as she pulled out a tray of cookies and placed them on the counter. As she removed them to the cooling rack and hummed, Analise, the college student who worked afternoons at the shop, gave her a dirty look and left the kitchen. Cynthia shrugged and went about her work.

She knew she annoyed many of the workers there with her constant good mood, but they didn't understand. She had a job for the first time in her life. A purpose, something to do that was all about making a better life for herself. There were still those moments that filled her with self-doubt. When her brother had stopped by a few weeks ago, she'd almost fallen apart. Thankfully, Max had been around and made sure Randall understood to leave her alone.

She wiped her brow with the back of her hand. Her hair, which she had stopped straightening, now curled around her face. Even though she wore a T-shirt that had fit her a few months ago, it now drew tight over her breasts, but that made it easier to work. The hip-hugger jeans were brand new. Through the weeks that followed her move, she'd stopped watching every little bit of food that went into her mouth. Without someone pointing out each ounce she gained, it was easy to savor food and no longer see it as the enemy. She'd always had a love/hate relationship with food, especially with the sweets she loved to bake. As each day passed, the bonds of her mother's catty comments dissolved. Granted, it meant she'd moved to a new size in clothing, but there was absolutely nothing normal about wearing zero and going to bed hungry each night.

With the high humidity and the heat of a Georgia summer in full swing, it promised to be a scorcher today, but she didn't care. She'd been up late last night talking to Chris. He called every few days and they talked—not about anything in particular, and they never really touched on sex or what had happened the night they spent together. But in the last month, she had gotten to know a lot about Chris Dupree, and what she did know she really liked. He cared for his family, was dedicated to his restaurant in Honolulu and made her want to be naughty. It was nothing he said. He hadn't made one sexual innuendo in all their conversations, but something about Chris made her want to misbehave.

"Looks like you're having a good day." Max leaned against the doorjamb, watching her work. She wondered how long he'd been standing there.

"Pretty good. How about you?"

"Well, it could be better. I had a meeting with your father early this morning."

She couldn't stop the pain that little comment brought. Her clothes had been delivered to Anna's house, and she had yet to speak to either of her parents. Even her mother had ignored the fact that her only daughter had turned thirty the week before.

"Why were you meeting with him?" Oh she hated the way her voice wavered. It made her sound like a frightened girl. And she wasn't.

Max's jaw flexed a couple of times, his eyes going cold. "We were supposed to discuss some business, but it turned nasty.

He made some remarks I didn't appreciate, and I told him I would not be doing business with him again."

"Oh no, I hope this has nothing to do with me, does it?" She would just die if she had caused Max any more problems.

"Indirectly. He made certain observations about Anna." From Max's thunderous look, Cynthia was pretty sure she knew what was said about Anna.

"Ah. Father isn't as bright as he claims to be."

Max's expression lightened. "No, he's not. Then he mentioned your grandmother's home in Hawaii. I didn't even pay attention to it until I got back to the office and did some checking. Do you have any idea about the state of your father's finances?"

She shook her head, puzzled. "No, why?"

He walked further into the kitchen. "It appears that your father is done up."

She laughed at first, thinking he was joking. When she realized he wasn't smiling, her laughter died. "My father is broke?"

"That's the rumor. I'm not sure if it's true or not, but I do know one thing. His temper has lost him a few contract bids with some big companies. He lost the Hilton job down in Boca Raton."

"That was a sure thing."

Max sighed and took her hand, leading her to a couple of barstools. Once they were both seated, he continued. "Your father has been losing credibility the last few years. But the thing I worry about is your trust."

"You don't have to worry about that. I got it several years ago, and it has been invested well."

"Are you sure?"

80

"I'm sure my money is safe."

He nodded. "That's good. What I have to worry about, though, is the mention of her home. Do you know why he would mention it?"

Frowning, she thought back. She'd only been eleven when her grandmother died, and she'd been devastated when the news reached her at summer camp. Her parents had forbidden her to accompany them to Hawaii for the funeral.

"No. All I knew about was the trust."

The timer went off for the cookies, and she rose to get them out of the oven. Once finished with the task, she turned to face him. "What do you think this is all about?"

He shook his head. "I'm really not sure. There are other rumors about your father. Some say his business dealings are not aboveboard."

"Father doesn't like to lose." It was sad to realize she didn't respect the man who had raised her. "I hate to say it, but I really think he wouldn't hesitate to break the law."

She hated dealing with things like this, but it was allowing her father to run over her for years that had gotten her where she was today. She had to start doing for herself.

Before she could even contemplate everything Max had told her and what it meant, her cell phone started ringing. It was her lawyer. "Cynthia. How are you doing?"

"Hello, Mr. Barton."

"I've had a situation arise, and I thought you should know about it. Your father told me he had your permission to sell off your grandmother's house in Hawaii."

"I don't understand. Why would he need my permission?"

There was a short silence, and she heard the squeak of his chair. "Cynthia, you do realize you inherited all her property in

Hawaii, don't you?"

"All of it?"

Papers rustled. "Yes, you own her house on the North Shore. I understood you visited her there a few times."

"Yes." Her knees had gone weak so she sat on the stool again. Max was looking at her, and he opened his mouth. She raised her hand to stop him. "Yes. I visited her there three summers prior to her death."

"You own that, along with a little land on Maui. That has condos on it, rentals for tourists. Also, you own a small but profitable macadamia nut farm. All of these to be transferred to you on your thirtieth birthday. I did try to contact you last week at your parents' home, but I have since learned you moved out."

She could almost feel the blood rush from her head, her mind spinning with the implications. "Yes, about a month ago."

"That's fine. I didn't have your cell phone number, but I had my assistant search, especially after the disturbing call from your father. He was trying to sell everything. And take the money that has accumulated."

"Accumulated?"

"Yes, as per your grandmother's request, we took the profits from the farm, rental property and her home—which has been rented out these past years—and invested it. You acquired it all."

"But...she left me a trust."

He paused as if trying to word his next comment just right. "Cynthia, I know you know there was no love lost between your grandmother and father. She had actually claimed she would disown her own daughter over the marriage, but she relented, thinking family was more important. But she did not trust him.

Your brother was given a trust also, but she claimed him to be a miniature image of your father. She refused to give him more. From what I know, he has already wasted all his money. The Hawaiian properties are yours, you just need to come by the office in Valdosta and sign some papers."

After setting up an appointment for the next morning, Cynthia hung up. By that point, Anna had joined them, her eyes as worried as Max's.

Anna took hold of her hands. "Cynthia. What is it?"

"I own it all."

Both of them studied her. Then Anna said, under her breath, "She's had some kind of shock."

"No." Cynthia pulled her hands free, her body finally coming back to life. "No. I'm fine. It seems there's a reason my father mentioned the property in Hawaii."

Walking away from them to the tray of cookies, she began to move them to the cooling rack. She needed something to keep herself busy.

"Last week I turned thirty."

There was a beat of silence. "Yes. We know that, Cynthia," Max said in a voice that someone might use with a lunatic he was afraid of. "We threw you a party."

She nodded, trying to gain some control over the emotions tumbling through her. Shock registered first; that was to be expected. But the next that came was sadness. Her parents had not only ignored her birthday, they were trying to figure out a way to steal from her. But the one thing that surprised her was the anger.

It began in her chest, white-hot and boiling. Until breaking off her engagement with Max, she'd done everything they expected. The right parties, the right boyfriends, the right friends. *Can't wear red lipstick, Cynthia; you'll look like a tramp. You're eating too much, Cynthia. You'll gain weight.*

And now they were trying to steal from her.

"Cynthia?" Anna approached her and pulled her into her arms when she saw the tears. "What is it?"

"I own everything my grandmother had in Hawaii. I'm apparently well off, besides the trust fund."

She drew back, and Anna studied her. "Why are you so sad?"

"I'm not sad. I'm pissed off. He was trying to sell it off. Stealing from his own daughter, the bastard."

"Oh, Cynthia." Pity filled Anna's voice, but for once Cynthia didn't give a damn. She allowed Anna to tug her back into an embrace. And she sobbed. Loud, horrible sobs that should have embarrassed her, but she didn't care. She was through with all the pretense, with all the lies and mistakes.

From now on, she would do what she damn well pleased.

Cynthia stared at the darkened windows of the tattoo parlor and pulled her bottom lip between her teeth. The storefront didn't appear particularly inviting, even if it was in a nice strip mall next to a used-clothing store.

Anna leaned close and whispered in Cynthia's ear, "It won't bite you."

Cynthia sighed. "I know."

Straightening away, Anna looked at the shop, then at Cynthia. "You were the one who brought up the idea of a tattoo. I can give you another present, like a round-trip ticket to

Hawaii," she said, humor lacing her voice.

Cynthia smiled. "I know."

"You don't have to do this if you don't want to."

But she wanted to. Anna had suggested a spa day just for the two of them. Cynthia had had other ideas. A tiny little spurt of rebellion that was now rapidly shrinking because she was scared of the tattoo parlor. That one thought had her straightening her shoulders.

She narrowed her eyes as she studied a young man who exited the shop. His arms were covered with an explosion of vivid colors.

"No, I don't have to, but I want to do it."

"Well, it's now or never, woman." Anna clamped her hand around Cynthia's upper arm and tugged her down the sidewalk to the front door.

When Anna pulled the door open, a bell tinkled overhead. The sound was at odds in the shop, which was not small and dingy as she had expected. The walls were covered with pictures to choose from, the track lighting overhead bright and almost blinding. When she glanced around the waiting area, she noticed a young couple with more interest in each other than anyone else, sitting in the corner, apparently waiting their turn.

Anna only gave Cynthia a minute to take in her surroundings before she dragged her to the counter.

"Hey, John. How's business been?"

Someone stepped out of what Cynthia assumed was an office. A man about her age was studying both her and Anna with interest. Average height, a bit stocky, he wore one of those tops that Anna called a wife-beater shirt. He leaned against the counter, his arms decorated much like the others she'd seen earlier. She watched, fascinated by the flexing of the muscle beneath the thin fabric and the way it made the dragon painted there move.

"Hey, doll. Going pretty good, considering summer is slow for me once the college kids blow town."

Anna nodded. "If I didn't get some influx with the new military moves at my Valdosta shop, it would probably hurt me just as much." She turned to Cynthia. "Cynthia, I would like you to meet John Gregory. John, Cynthia would like to get her first tattoo."

The smile she offered him froze the moment she made eye contact with him.

"Really?" The disbelief she heard in his voice was mirrored in his eyes as he studied her. He cocked his head to one side, causing one of the streams of light to reflect on his head.

At first, she faltered. What the hell was she thinking? A Myers didn't get a tattoo. A Myers wouldn't know where they did tattoos let alone contemplate what she wanted printed on her ass. Her mother would keel over if she knew. Anna must have sensed Cynthia's hesitation because she gave her a nudge.

She cleared her throat as a wave of heat filled her face. John's lips curved into a knowing smile. The action sent indignant irritation inching down her spine. It blocked out every one of her insecurities. Being the good girl sucked, and she was sick and tired of it.

She stepped forward and smiled. "Yes. Anna told me you're the best in the area."

The smile he offered her was at best smarmy, at worse feral. She didn't look like someone who would come in here, so what?

"Do you have a problem with that, Mr...er...John?"

Even she winced at the primness in her voice. Goodness,

she sounded as if she were at a garden party at the country club. The urge to run started to thrum louder through her blood until John snorted and crossed his arms over his chest. The rude sound and gesture caused her impatience to increase.

"I just figured with your reputation, this might be a little out of your league."

The fact that he knew her didn't surprise Cynthia. In their small town, most people were familiar with the Myers family since they employed a huge chunk of the population. Being associated with her father definitely wouldn't win her any friends. He had a reputation of being a hard ass, firing people at will. Her mother had probably offended most working people in town, and her brother had a habit of picking fights with people he thought too weak to win.

And, truthfully, John had a point. A week ago, she would have turned with her tail between her legs and run away. But this was the *new* Cynthia Myers, and she was not backing down from the things she had always yearned to do. From the time she was in college, she had wanted a little bitty heart-shaped tattoo on her rear end and by God, it was going to happen.

Straightening her spine and stepping forward, she said, in her mother's condescending voice, "I'll tell you what, *John*, how about you let me worry about my reputation, and you get ready to draw a pretty little pink heart on my ass."

Anna snorted behind her, but Cynthia ignored her. Lord knew she had gained the attention of the young couple because she had enunciated every word quite loudly. She kept her focus on John, whose face was as blank as newly rolled pie dough, and waited for him to challenge her. If he did, she had no idea what she would say to rebut him but she would come up with something.

Instead of giving her more crap—Anna was really becoming a bad influence on her language—John smiled. This time, though, the smile was wide and friendly, his eyes twinkling. "You got it, Cynthia."

While the couple who had been waiting followed him back, Cynthia filled out paperwork and release forms. By the time she was laid out on a table with her butt bared, Cynthia started to regret her bravado. It was one thing to be brave in the face of criticism from a man she didn't know. It was completely different having him study her rear.

"I think you should do another color." Anna stood off to the right of her, apparently having no problem with the situation. Of course, it wasn't her body on display. "I think red would be better."

Cynthia fought back the growl that threatened to escape. "I heard you the first three times you said it."

Anna grunted and turned around to study some books John said had tattoo pictures in them. Cynthia sighed and relaxed until John spoke again.

"I need to get the stencil on here and I can start the line work."

"Uh-huh."

He pressed a piece of paper against the fullest part of her right cheek and pulled it away.

"Looks good." He turned away from her and started to assemble his tools. "Do you want to see it in a mirror, to check the placement?"

"No."

He paused. "Are you sure you want this? Right now, this isn't permanent."

She hesitated and nodded. "I want the tattoo."

"Okay. It's your ass."

Cynthia gritted her teeth, closed her eyes and tried to remind herself that this was what she wanted.

❧

"I can't believe you took her to get a tattoo," Max growled as he frowned at Anna.

Cynthia stifled a sigh and shifted her weight against the padded seat. He'd been in a mood since he found out where Cynthia and Anna had spent their afternoon.

"Cynthia is her own woman, Max." Anna showed no reaction to his threatening tone as she sipped her sweet tea. Even after all the time she spent in their company, Cynthia was still amazed at how easily Anna dealt with Max.

When she noticed Max's face turning red, she decided to step in. "It was my decision."

He grunted. "Anna can be very persuasive."

"Actually, Maxwell, we got off cheap. I offered Cynthia a round-trip ticket to Hawaii."

Before Max could form a retort, the waitress showed back up to take their food orders. Once they were alone, he started in on them again. "It isn't as if Cynthia came up with the tattoo idea on her own. You can be a bad influence."

They continued to bicker. Cynthia watched them from across the table as a whisper of annoyance slipped down her spine. They were discussing her as if she weren't there and had no say-so in her actions. It was just too much for someone trying her best to break free.

She cleared her throat and was ignored. The rebellious anger that had been boiling beneath her skin since she dumped

Max bubbled over. Deciding she had heard more than enough, she interrupted them with one comment. "I've decided to go to Hawaii for a few months."

Both Anna and Max stopped their argument and turned to stare at her. Truthfully, Cynthia had doubts about her decision. It wasn't like her to make so many life-altering decisions in one day. First she got her butt tattooed and now she was moving thousands of miles away. She might have lost her mind, but damn it felt good.

Max was the first one to gain his footing. "Months? How long?"

She shrugged. The idea of moving there permanently scared her. At the same time, she felt a thrum of excitement she hadn't felt in quite some time.

"You can't just pick up and move." Max's tone told her that he had made the decision and it would be followed.

"Actually," she said with a defiant smile, "I can."

Anna coughed, drawing Cynthia's attention. A gleam of amusement twinkled in her eyes.

"She's got you there, Max." Anna cocked her head to one side. "What are you planning on doing when you get there...or should I ask who?"

"I'm not sure."

"Why would you want to go there?" Max asked.

"Again, I'm not really sure. I just know that those were some of the happiest times of my life. My grandmother loved it there, and since the house is free, I figured a few months there to plan out what I want to do with the rest of my life would be good."

Max's frown returned. "I don't like it."

"Really? I wouldn't have guessed. What I don't understand

is why you think it's your business."

That question caught him off guard because, for the first time in all the years she had known him, Max seemed to be at a loss for words.

"I've been thinking about this since last week. I want to go, it's my choice to go, and for once in my life, I'm doing what I want to do."

"Fantastic," Anna said. "Have you told Chris?"

Max glowered at Anna. "Chris? Why would she tell him? She met him once at our wedding—"

"She did more than that."

"*Anna.*" Heat crept up Cynthia's neck. "Stop trying to bait Max."

"You didn't answer my question," Max said, ignoring their byplay.

"No, you two are the first I've told."

Max pursed his lips and studied her. He opened his mouth but the waitress returned with their salads, and he again waited for her to leave.

This time, when he spoke, Max's voice held a gentler tone. "You haven't told your family?"

Shame and embarrassment swamped her. She had never had much of a relationship with her parents. Even as a child she didn't fit in with them. Her brother seemed to always know what her father wanted. No matter what he did, Randall didn't get punished. *Boys will be boys.* Randall was still a boy.

Her life had been filled with etiquette lessons, dance rehearsals and debutante balls. Not once had anyone ever asked her if she wanted those things, they just expected it. They hadn't cared that she'd thrown up all day before her dance performances, or that most of the young men they allowed her to date made her skin crawl. She had done it out of some kind of misguided loyalty…because they were family.

And now they wanted nothing to do with her, except the fact they wanted her money.

Shaking herself free of her depressing thoughts, she picked up her fork to dig into her salad. "No. My father is not speaking to me, you know that. Once he realized my grandmother's properties were off limits, he probably threw a fit. You know what kind of temper he has."

Anna reached across the table and patted her hand. "I have to say I feel honored that you told us first. When are you planning to leave and just what the hell am I going to do without you?"

"Way to worry about Cynthia," Max quipped.

Cynthia bit her lip and then laughed, rather loudly. "I really love you two."

Both of them stared at her with blank expressions.

"What? You don't believe me?"

Anna blinked rapidly. "It's just an odd thing to hear from your husband's ex-fiancée."

"I do love you guys. Most of my acquaintances have disappeared, refused to return phone calls because they think I don't have my daddy's money. But you stuck by me."

"Of course I did. No one can make a macadamia nut biscotti like you."

"Anna, stop." Max looked at Cynthia. His demeanor had calmed, and he smiled for the first time since hearing about their trip to John's Tattoo. "She's trying to tell you that we love you too."

Cynthia sniffed and blinked, hoping she didn't start crying in front of them and the whole happy hour crowd. She heard a sniffle from Anna.

Max cleared his throat. "Why don't we discuss when and how you're going to move over there?"

Cynthia zipped the last piece of luggage, mentally going over her checklist. She had an early start to the morning, and she really didn't want to leave anything behind. She'd packed all her cooking gear, and Anna said she would ship that as soon as Cynthia got her mail set up. As she looked around the bedroom, she felt a bit sad about leaving. She hadn't lived in Anna's house long, but it held a special place in her heart. It had been the first step she'd taken for her independence.

The doorbell rang and she smiled, thinking that Anna must have decided to come back to talk more. When she opened the door, she found she'd been terribly wrong.

Chapter Seven

"Hello, Cynthia, do you mind if I come in?"

Maryanne Myers had been considered a catch in her younger years, and would still be today. Perfectly dressed in an unwrinkled linen suit, not a hair out of place, and her makeup unsmudged—even at nine o'clock at night—she remained a handsome woman. Naturally, the eyelift and chin tuck she'd had last year in anticipation of being Mother of the Bride helped.

"No, of course not, Mother."

She closed the door and they stood staring at each other. Many people had told her through the years she resembled her mother, and she guessed she did in a way. Both were small boned, blonde and fair skinned. While her mother had hazel eyes, Cynthia had inherited her coloring from her father. Two months ago, they'd had a lot more in common. The outfit she wore was one Cynthia could have borrowed, and the straightened hair was in almost the same exact style she used to keep. Looking at her mother, Cynthia realized she had dodged a bullet. While beautiful, her mother rarely showed emotion and never truly smiled.

The silence stretched, becoming uncomfortable. Knowing that it was probably going to be that way until her mother left, she decided to move things along.

Waving her hand in the direction of the kitchen, she said, "Why don't we talk in the kitchen."

After her mother was settled at the kitchen table, Cynthia sat opposite of her, purposely not offering her any refreshment. It took every bit of her control not to, because those damned manners had been drilled into her head. It was juvenile to act that way, but her mother didn't deserve to be offered anything.

"What do you want, Mother?"

The sigh her mother let loose was one Cynthia had heard most of her life. Whenever she missed a step in dance, whenever she embarrassed them with her childish outbursts of laughter, her mother sighed like that. In that one little action, she let her daughter know just how much of a disappointment she was to her and the family.

"I heard that you are moving."

Cynthia fought the kernel of hope that sprang to life. Was it possible her mother wanted to mend the fences?

"Yes."

"Are you planning on staying at your grandmother's?"

"Yes, I am." She studied her mother and noted the nervousness in her gaze. "Why are you really here?"

"I found out from Janice Hoffmockle that you were moving. I cannot believe you did not inform us. I had to find out from a woman who cleans homes."

The disdain in her voice aggravated Cynthia. It always had. Her mother had come from money, but Cynthia's grandfather had earned it through hard work, unlike her father who had inherited it. Maryanne Myers thought herself better than a woman who held an honest job. Instead of confronting her mother, she ground her teeth.

"When Father told me to leave, and you agreed, I decided

95

that there was no reason for contacting you."

The frown her mother offered her was another gesture Cynthia was familiar with. "So, you are going to take over the family assets in Hawaii."

Pain speared her heart. She would never defy her father and reach out to her daughter. "They aren't *family* owned. They're mine."

"Your father was planning on using those holdings for investments."

For several moments, Cynthia said nothing. She couldn't. Parents were supposed to protect their children, wish the best for them. Hers still saw her as a means to an end. She wanted to weep, but she would never show that weakness in front of her mother. Instead, she hardened her expression.

"Funny, because all along you two knew that money was mine. Was this a plan all along, or did you just come up with it on the fly?"

"On the fly? Where on earth did you learn such an expression?"

"Does it really matter, Mother? Just tell me what Father sent you here to say."

Her mother seemed surprised by Cynthia's bluntness, her face losing all expression. She recovered fast enough, her eyes snapping with anger, her voice dripping with disdain. "You've been spending time with that tramp. Have you no pride? She stole your husband."

Cynthia almost laughed at the absurdity of her mother's statement, but she couldn't find enough humor to even smile. "He wasn't my husband, he wasn't even my fiancé at the time. Max would have been a horrible match for me."

Her mother waved away the argument. "What I want to

know is, are you going to help your father out?"

"Help him out?"

"He's run into a bit of a cash-flow problem."

"So, he sent you here to beg for my help."

Her mother's spine stiffened even more. "I will not beg you for anything. What I came here to do was appeal to your family honor."

Now Cynthia did laugh, but there was no humor in it. The ache in her chest spread through her, chilling her from the inside out.

"Family honor? What the hell do the Myers know about honor?"

"Cynthia Louisa Myers, your father has sacrificed a lot for you over the years."

"Not near as much as I have."

"I have no idea why you think you deserve all that money, that land, but my misguided mother thought it a big joke. And what have you done to deserve it? You couldn't even keep a man long enough to marry him."

Anger now replaced the hurt and she used it to lash out. "Touché. But then, I didn't want to spend my life married to a man I didn't love, turning a blind eye to his affairs, pretending that everything was fine."

A flash of something that could have been pain came and went in her mother's eyes. Shame filled her and she opened her mouth to apologize, but her mother stopped her with a comment.

"And what do you have now? You've let yourself go, and for what? You have your independence but you have no man, no one to lean on."

"Not that I think you ever had that with Father, but I don't need a man to support me. If I find one, one I truly love, he will accept me for who I am and would never cheat on me."

Her mother shook her head. "You think your father and I don't know where you spent the night of Max's wedding? Please." She sniffed. "I didn't raise you to go slumming with the first man you could pick up."

Cynthia refused to defend her actions. She had done nothing wrong. "I want you to leave."

Her mother's eyes widened and then narrowed before she stood. "This is your last chance at rebuilding any kind of relationship with your father."

"What about you?"

"I agree with your father. You have to do what is right for the family."

The hope Cynthia'd had earlier was now shriveled and dead. What the hell had she been thinking, that her mother would actually come to her because she cared about her daughter? Rising to her feet, she faced her mother squarely.

The burning ball of pain in her stomach she had not had since moving out of her parents' house returned. She pressed her hand against her tummy, hoping her ulcer was not resurfacing. "If the relationship comes with the prerequisite that I hand over my money, I think I can do without those ties."

"If that is what you want."

"It's not what I want, it's what I have been stuck with for too long. If you all want a regular relationship, then contact my lawyer, other than that, leave me the hell alone."

She shook her head at Cynthia. "You've lost any kind of manners and class I taught you. Your father was right. You *are* useless."

The need to curl up in a ball and cry almost overwhelmed

her but she pushed it back, knowing that later she would have the time for that. "I'm not the one who had to beg her daughter for money." Her mother opened her mouth to shoot back, but Cynthia had had enough. "Just go. I don't need any more dramatic statements from you. Be sure to tell Father that from now on, not to send you to do the dirty work. Tell him to be a man and do it himself."

With a look of contempt, her mother turned on her heel and left. Cynthia held on until she heard the door click shut and the car pull out of the driveway. Then she sat back down at the table, rested her head on her arms and wept.

Chris cursed under his breath when he dropped the salt shaker he was filling and it spewed salt all over the table. Sighing, he began to clean up the mess and tried to get his emotions settled. It had been a bitch of a week. Three of his waitstaff were sick—flu—and he was sure others would follow soon enough. On top of that, his manager had broken her ankle and was out for the rest of the week, doctor's orders. So he was covering shifts, doing extra work, when he really wanted to be on the phone with Cynthia.

Pathetic. Every day he counted the hours until he spoke to her, and today it had been pushed back thanks to the workload. If he could avoid his family's calls, he would be finished. But his brother had called twice and his mother three times, and if he'd ignored those calls, they would've called over and over until he answered.

"Chris?"

He turned and found Lee, one of his hostesses, standing a little too close. Since his manager, Maylea, had hired her, Lee, a petite redhead, had made no secret of the fact that she wanted to fuck him. Chris never fucked the help, it only led to disaster. But truth was, he wasn't interested—in anyone. Other than Cynthia. He didn't need to deal with the woman the waitstaff had named "the Barracuda".

"What do you need?" He stepped around the table with the pretense of cleaning up more salt.

"Kaile called. He can't work. Another case of the flu."

He exhaled. "Do we have anyone to work in his place?"

"I called Denise. She said she can make it, but she'll be thirty minutes late. She's waiting for a sitter."

He nodded. "Thanks, Lee."

She began to turn around, but then paused, looking back over her shoulder. "Since we're both working late, maybe we should get a drink after we close up."

For a second he studied her—well rounded, with beautiful green eyes, a full, pouty mouth, a pair of breasts that had to have been bought and paid for—and felt...nothing.

"You know I don't date the staff."

She frowned. "I don't know why you have to be such a saint." With that she marched away, her full ass swinging with each step.

"I'd watch out for angry women, Chris."

He glanced over and found his friend Evan Chambers smiling at him. "Hey, whatcha doing here so early?"

"Finished my meeting early."

Evan was about eighteen months younger than Chris. He'd started with nothing, just like Chris, working construction. Now he owned one of the most successful construction companies in Hawaii. With his gray eyes and golden-brown hair, Evan had captured and bedded more than one of Chris's employees.

"We're short of staff, so be warned, I might put you to work."

Evan smiled, then glanced over at Lee, who was talking to one of the waitresses. "If you put me to work on that one, I'll do just fine. Don't you just want to bend her over and fuck that ass?"

"Evan, I can't talk about staff that way. You know that. Did you need something?"

"Nope. I was meeting with Daniel Akita. He's redoing the shop." Evan sat at one of the chairs at a neighboring table, watching as Chris moved to fill another salt dispenser. "You seem out of sorts."

"The flu has hit Dupree's with a vengeance. I'll be pulling some longer–than–normal days this week."

"No. You've been distracted since you returned from the mainland."

He wanted to deny it. He hadn't talked to anyone about Cynthia. Keeping her a secret hadn't been his goal, but his feelings for her were too new, too...raw. Talking about her would've revealed things he hadn't been ready to face. Still wasn't. Looking at Evan, he realized he wouldn't get out of it. Having close friends was a bitch.

"I met a woman."

Evan chuckled. "So what's new? Fuck her, get her out of your system."

Chris sighed, wishing Evan weren't so cynical, but knowing his tragic background, Chris understood. "I did. Several times." He paused as he topped off a salt shaker. "I think I found the one."

Evan didn't react at first. Both of them had lived the lifestyle at one time—Evan was still involved. He understood

Chris's problems, of his status and why he had left.

Evan frowned. "The one? As in a woman who can handle a switch?"

As he finished up with the salt, Chris nodded toward his office door. "Let's take this back there. Don't want gossip."

When they were in the privacy of his office, Chris settled into his chair behind the desk, and Evan sat in one of the chairs situated in front. "Now, tell me about this woman."

"She's not my type at all. Buttoned down, at least until you get her in the bedroom." He closed his eyes as the memories rolled over him. As if she were there, he could taste her skin, smell her arousal, remember the way it felt as her pussy clenched around his cock.

"She's a switch? The one you've been looking for?"

Chris didn't miss the disbelief in Evan's voice. He opened his eyes and found his friend studying him.

"She doesn't realize it. But I let her lead, and I could see it. You know what I mean. Jesus, Evan, every time she took control, she got off on it."

Evan rubbed his chin. "Does she know about you?"

"That I'm a switch? She doesn't even know what one is, let alone that I am one, or that she is."

"Chris, I'll just say be careful. I thought you'd never... Well, after what happened, I thought you'd never have anything to do with the lifestyle again."

Chris's mind drifted back three years earlier, to Jasmine. Gorgeous, big-boned, dark hair, beautiful blue eyes. He didn't look past the beauty to see the problems beneath the surface. She'd convinced him she wanted to be a switch, but in the end she couldn't even handle being a sub, let alone taking the dominant role. She wanted total submission—to be a slave. It wasn't in Chris to give it to her. In the end, she left him, and three months later she'd committed suicide. After her death, Chris had found out she'd been unstable for years, but he still blamed himself for not realizing earlier she had problems.

"I know, but it has nothing to do with the lifestyle. It has more to do with what she needs. At the moment, she needs to be in control, to be the one calling the shots. If you met her, you'd understand."

"If I met her, I could get her into bed in a heartbeat, fuck her until she couldn't walk, and she would forget all about you."

Chris smiled, shaking his head. "No. Once you meet her, you'll understand. Of course, if it goes as I plan, I might need your help."

Evan nodded, and Chris knew he understood. They talked for a few more minutes, then Evan left Chris alone. Chris glanced up at the clock and realized he had just enough time to call Cynthia. With the time difference, he had to call her in the middle of the afternoon or it would be too late when he got home.

He locked his office door and dialed her cell phone number. As he waited for her to answer, the same familiar energy surged through him, his body pulsing with it. It had been killing him to keep the conversations light. And to make it worse, for the last three weeks or so, she'd seemed preoccupied. Something was going on, but he was trying his best not to pry.

"Hello." Soft, southern, sexy.

"Hello, *chéri*. How are you doing?"

She paused for just a second, as if deciding whether she should tell him something. Then she continued. "I'm doing fine. I've been super busy today."

"Same here. Have a few people out with the flu, so I'm working late tonight."

"That's too bad." Another pause. "Chris?"

"Yes, *chéri?*"

"I have something to ask you, something I want you to be completely truthful about."

"Okay. Go ahead."

He heard her swallow and then take a deep breath. Anticipation skated along his nerves as he wondered what could be bothering her so much.

"When you were here, and we spent the night together…"

"Yes?" His heart pounded.

"Well, it's just that, you don't… When you were here, you couldn't keep your hands off me, and now you act like a…a…*brother.*" Again, she drew in a deep breath and asked, "Please, just let me know, Chris. Are you not interested in me that way anymore?"

Chapter Eight

For several seconds, Chris didn't say anything. Couldn't. It was amazing that she actually would think he wasn't interested. What was going through her mind?

"Cynthia, *chéri*...you know I'm interested in you."

"No, I don't."

"I think I proved that six weeks ago."

"Then...yes. But it has been six weeks, and you haven't once said a word about it."

He drew in a fortifying breath, trying to gather his control. Just talking to her on the phone had him hard, and since it had been six weeks since he'd touched her, touched any woman, it wouldn't take much to get him off.

"Honey, it's just that I didn't know when we would see each other again. So I avoided it."

"You avoided talking about it because you don't plan to see me for a while?" Now she didn't sound upset, but confused.

"You don't understand."

"Explain it to me then. When you were here, you said you couldn't get enough of me. But for some reason, I think you have."

"Well I haven't. I never will. Listen, Cynthia, I can't talk about it." Already, he was stroking himself through his pocket.

Sad and pathetic, but talking about that night, even the smallest mention, made him hard.

"Are there people around?"

"No. I'm by myself. It's just that..." Telling her would let her know just how much control she had over him, how much she meant to him. He didn't want to scare her away, but she wasn't going to let it go. "If I were to talk about it, I'd have to get off. There's just no way around it."

He heard her breath catch. The sound was as arousing as the sound of her moans. "So, right now, you're..."

"Hard enough to drive a nail into cement."

There was a long pause. "Are you touching yourself right now?" Her voice bubbled with excitement, her Southern accent deepening.

Damn. The woman was going to be the death of him. He leaned his head back against the chair and closed his eyes, praying for some sort of control. "Yes."

"You're naked?" Her pleasure spurred his.

"No. I'm stroking over the fabric."

Then she said something he never would have expected. "Take your cock out."

His eyes flew open, and he almost dropped the phone. "What?"

"Take it out."

Chris seriously thought about denying her. Definitely not the place to do this. But there was something in the way she'd ordered him that had him reacting to her demand. He unbuttoned and unzipped his pants, and pushed the fabric aside. His erection bobbed free once he pulled down his underwear a bit. He grabbed it by the base and stroked.

"Does that feel good?" Her tone had turned coy.

"Yessss."

"Are you stroking yourself?"

"Yes."

"Hmm, I wish I were there. I liked having your cock in my hand...in my mouth."

Jesus. A rush of heat pumped to his cock and left his balls aching. He shifted his weight, leaning back. Remembering what was going on and where he was, he grabbed the towel on his desk and placed it over his shirt.

"Are you about to come?"

"No."

"That's good. I'm lying here naked. I had a nightshirt on when you called, but I can't help touching myself when I hear your voice."

He had died and gone to heaven. Holy God. "Tell me more. Tell me what you want me to do, what you would like to do."

"I wish you were here. Then I could have your hands on me."

"Hmmm." He was getting close.

"Don't come yet, Chris. I'm not there yet. I'm wet, but...not there."

Oh Lord, she was masturbating with him. This was something he never expected, and for that reason alone it was doubly arousing.

"Are you still stroking?"

"Yes."

"You know what I want? I want to taste you again. I want to take your cock in my mouth, suck you, lick you." With each comment, her voice had grown thinner, breathier. He could tell she was close. "I'd love to have your mouth on my...pussy.

Eating me while I suck you."

He curled his toes inside his shoes, trying to hold off like she asked, but it was getting harder by the second. Every nerve in his body was on alert, the tension growing, stretching him thinner. He imagined her spread out on her bed, her hand on that pretty pussy, her fingers slipping into herself.

"Oh, yes. Yes. Baby. Chris, honey, now. Come now."

He was already pumping himself, driving toward his orgasm. His balls tightened, his head spun. The next instant, he exploded.

"Cynthia!"

He continued to pump as he blew his load. The hot liquid landed on the towel he'd laid on his stomach as his body went rigid. Slowly, he relaxed, his muscles now weak from the exertion. He closed his eyes, his body gradually coming down. For several moments, the only sound on the line was their heavy breathing.

"Cynthia?"

"Yes, Chris?" Her voice held no embarrassment, no recriminations. Just complete and utter satisfaction.

"I would have tried this six weeks ago if I had known you were into phone sex."

She laughed. The sound had him smiling. He had a feeling she didn't laugh that often, and each time he heard the sweet sound, something shifted in his chest.

"I've never been before."

He opened his eyes and noticed the time. "Damn, honey, I gotta get back to work. Dinner rush is about to start."

"I understand. And I have to get to bed."

"I'll give you a call tomorrow."

"Hmm." She paused. "I might be out of range about this

time tomorrow, but I'll call you back if you miss me."

"Okay. Night, Cynthia."

"Night."

After disconnecting, he cleaned himself up, his mind still turning over the comment she'd made at the end. He zipped his pants and discarded the towel. She'd never been unreachable before, always seemed to have her cell with her, and he couldn't stop the nagging feeling she was keeping something from him. Someone knocked on the door, and his worries were pushed aside as the dinner crowd started to arrive.

Cynthia lay in her hotel bedroom thinking she should be embarrassed. Sweat had gathered between her breasts, her heart was still beating out of control, and she hadn't felt this relaxed in weeks. For some reason, having phone sex with Chris felt right. Two months ago, if someone had told her she would be having phone sex with a man she'd had a one-night stand with, she would have said they were mental.

She pulled her nightshirt over her head and settled back in bed. Her flight was early in the morning, and now she was wide awake. Turning on the TV, she decided to find something to put her to sleep. Eleven hours from Atlanta to Honolulu.

The last three and a half weeks had been a whirlwind of activity. Once she'd signed the papers, she'd taken over all her grandmother's properties in Hawaii. She'd stayed two weeks in Lake Park, helping Anna with her newly hired baker.

Waiting had almost killed her, but she hadn't wanted to leave Anna high and dry. And Cynthia needed to get her affairs in order. The people who had been renting her grandmother's house had just vacated. Perfect timing.

She wanted to see Chris. The timing was convenient, but she'd waited because she worried about her feelings for him.

Even though she had tried her best not to, she'd become attached to him and, apparently, would go to any lengths to please him. She'd never had phone sex and had never masturbated. Ever. And she had done both because the sound of his voice, the fact that he was aroused and touching himself...it had been too much to ignore. Even as she blushed, she couldn't feel guilty.

Lord only knew what kind of trouble she would get into in Hawaii. But she was looking forward to every minute of it.

Chapter Nine

The scent of plumeria intermingled with the spicy scents of Dupree's as Cynthia walked up the path to the front door. The sun was setting behind her, and she breathed in another dose of heavy Hawaiian air. Dusk was her favorite time in Hawaii. The heat of the day disappeared, leaving a clean, crisp feeling to the air. The restaurant wasn't too far off Kalakaua Boulevard, close to the heart of Waikiki, but even in the heart of the city, the area was unpolluted. It was something she loved about Hawaii.

A lot of people waited for tables, lingering around the benches in front. Jazz poured from the speakers, not too loud, but just loud enough to let you appreciate the music. She gained a few looks when she passed a group of men. These were not the type of men who paid attention to her, usually. They were attractive, but almost too attractive, and they knew it. But she'd dressed in a pair of low-riding, hip-hugging jeans, a snug T-shirt and sandals. She was sure the red lipstick and out-of-control curls, thanks to the Hawaiian humidity, had something to do with it. Smiling to herself, she reached for the front door, only to have another dangerously good-looking man open it for her.

This one was pure sex. Gray eyes, with a hint of blue, along with golden-brown hair, he had to be taller than Chris, who was just over six feet.

"Thank you."

"The pleasure is all mine. Do I note a little of the South in your voice?" His voice was deep, Southern and filled with sensual teasing.

She nodded, but said nothing else as she stepped over the threshold. Although attractive, he was a hunter, and that wasn't what she wanted. She dismissed him from her mind the moment she entered Chris's restaurant, which was decorated in bold splashes of color, with scenes from New Orleans in pictures and murals on the walls. The jazz that played outside lingered, but at a much more muted volume. The lighting was subdued, the waiters and waitresses dressed in red and black. The aroma she'd first encountered outside almost overpowered her within the cozy confines of the restaurant. A mixture of spices, peppers and onions scented the air in the room.

"May I help you?"

A young woman stood behind a podium, or rather, leaned on crutches behind the podium. With her gold skin, high cheekbones and wide nose, it was clear the woman was Hawaiian, but her most distinctive feature was her eyes. They were the most amazing shade of blue. Piled on top of her head, her hair was black, smooth and probably went down to her waist. Not a stitch of makeup adorned her face, nor did she need it.

"I hope you can. I was looking for Chris."

"She appears to be the sweet magnolia Chris met when he went to the mainland."

She jumped at the voice of the man she'd encountered at the front door.

"Evan." The woman behind the podium had gone breathless when she said the man's name, but then cleared her throat. She looked up at him, admiration—no, beyond admiration—in her eyes. Cynthia knew a cynic when she saw one. Evan was one, and this woman would probably get hurt in the end.

The oblivious male smiled at the woman as though she were his little sister. "May, how are you doing? Chris said you had an accident."

May blushed. "Nothing big." May returned her attention to Cynthia. Cynthia sensed the young woman fighting the urge to sneak a glance at Evan. "Chris is a bit busy, but I can take you into the back."

"Oh...I don't want you to go to any trouble."

May laughed, the sound of it turning a few heads, including several men. It was one of the most lyrical sounds Cynthia had ever heard.

"Get me away from this podium. Chris stuck me here." As the woman hobbled down the hall, she said over her shoulder, "The doctor ordered me to stay home, but I knew Chris needed my help."

"He's lucky to have you."

She laughed again. "I have a feeling he would argue with you tonight." She stopped at a set of chrome doors. Cynthia hurried to open them. "Thanks. Still learning how to do that since I've only been on these suckers for two days."

As soon as she entered the kitchen, Cynthia saw Chris. Her heart did the little flip-flop she never seemed able to control. Her nerves stretched thinner. What would she do if he rejected her? What would she do if he didn't?

Nothing could diminish how good he looked. Chopping vegetables at one of the workstations, he was joking with a young man beside him. Dressed in jeans and a T-shirt with the Dupree's logo splashed across it in red, Chris laughed, the

113

sound making her smile.

May approached him, and he stopped laughing, his eyes narrowing on the young woman. He settled his hands on his hips. "Maylea, I told you to stay up on the stool. I'll fire you if I find you on your feet again."

"And then you would have to close Dupree's. Besides, I brought you a present, bruddah."

She gestured in Cynthia's direction. When Chris shifted his attention from May to her, his expression froze for just a second. Everyone else seemed to disappear, and all she could see was him. He said something; she thought it might be her name. In the next instant, he strode purposefully toward her. Her breath caught in her throat. Without a word, he pulled her into his arms. Immediately, his mouth was on hers, his tongue tangling with hers. He lifted her off the floor as she slid her arms up his, over his shoulders and around his neck. She wanted to wrap her legs around his waist. She wanted him naked. She wanted to be naked with him.

The hoots, whistles and clapping of the kitchen staff brought both of them back to the present. Chris broke the kiss, a wry grin curving his lips. Her heart was still pounding out of control. She couldn't seem to catch her breath, and the sensual hunger she witnessed in his eyes didn't help either. Slowly, oh so slowly, he slid her down his body and to the floor. But not before she felt his erection. He grimaced, and she laughed. Pulling her in front of him, he turned both of them toward their audience.

"Everyone, this is Cynthia. Cynthia, this is everyone."

Everyone smiled at them, except a little redhead in the back. She frowned, her expression vicious. Before Cynthia could ask who she was, Chris was pulling her out of the kitchen. He walked right past Evan, ignoring him when he said hi.

Chris didn't say another word. He allowed her to enter the office first, then closed and locked the door, leaning against it.

He smiled at her, still not saying anything.

"What? You're making me nervous."

His smile grew. "Just trying to take it in that you're here."

Joy curled into her heart at his words and the tone in his voice.

"If I would have known..." He frowned. "Why didn't you tell me you were coming yesterday?"

"I didn't want you to feel obligated. I actually had thought about waiting a few days before visiting you."

"You just got in?"

"Yeah. Well, I stopped by the house first, but I couldn't wait."

"House?"

"I'll tell you about all that later."

His gaze roamed over her. "You're looking good, *chéri*."

She threaded her hands through her hair. "A little bit of a change, huh?"

He nodded as he walked forward. Sliding his hands around her waist, he drew her against him, enveloping her in an embrace. The heat of his body warmed her and his scent surrounded her as he rested his chin on her head.

"How long is your visit?"

"I'm not sure yet. I have some things to sort out."

He leaned back. "What kind of things?"

"Well..." All of a sudden, she was nervous. She didn't know why, because her happiness didn't depend on Chris. She pulled away, and he let her go easily enough. Wandering around the

115

room, she tried to work up the nerve to tell him of her move.

"Cynthia, is there something you need to tell me?"

The seriousness in his voice caught her attention. She turned to face him. "Well, yes. It's all kind of complicated. I just want you to know that I'm not here to pressure you. I stopped by because..."

He stepped closer, placing his hands on her waist. "Because why?"

"I told you. I couldn't help myself. It's embarrassing, completely embarrassing, but after our night...and then last night..."

He smiled. "Yeah, that was definitely something."

She punched him, and he laughed. A knock at the door interrupted them. The door handle jiggled, and she thought she heard someone cuss. "Boss, we have a situation in the kitchen."

Chris didn't even turn around. "Be there in a minute, Lee."

Lee's sigh was audible through the door. "We need you now."

"And I said I will be there in a minute. I own the restaurant, so I think I can determine when I will get there."

There was a pregnant pause, then another disgusted sigh. Cynthia wasn't surprised to hear the woman stomp away.

"Chris..."

"Don't worry. Lee isn't going to be nice to you, so just avoid her." He bent his head and gave her a quick, hard kiss. "You want something to eat? You must be exhausted."

"A little tired, but I slept a lot on the trip over."

He nodded. "Can you give me about an hour?"

"Sure."

He kissed her again, and left her alone with her thoughts.

Chris broke up the argument two busboys were having over a woman neither would probably be able to handle, and helped with some more prep work. After that he went out into the restaurant, talked to guests, and made sure May was resting her ankle. He was anxious to get back to Cynthia—pathetic, but at this point there was nothing he could do about it.

Starting back to his office, he thought about the changes in her. It seemed that moving out of her parents' house had done her a world of good. She'd put on a few pounds, though she still needed more, and with her curly hair and casual attire, he'd been hard-pressed to keep his hands off her. In fact, it had been impossible. And now that she was in Hawaii...

His cock twitched. Where Cynthia was concerned, he had little or no control.

He saw Evan at the bar, flirting with the new female bartender. When his friend caught sight of him, he signaled him over. Knowing he had snubbed Evan earlier, Chris changed course and took a stool beside him.

"So, your magnolia showed up."

He didn't miss Evan's sarcasm, but he ignored it. "Yes."

Evan shot him a look, and Chris smiled. Evan rolled his eyes. "Good Lord, you're useless. You are definitely whipped."

"Happily. You saw her."

Evan took a long pull off his beer bottle before answering. "You think this is the one?"

Chris grabbed a few nuts. "No, she *is* the one. I can feel it."

"You can feel it? Fuck, you sound like you've been listening to Dr. Phil. Women are never to be trusted—you should know that. Believe me, I learned that at an early enough age."

Chris understood why Evan detested women, where the

117

deep-rooted hatred came from, but it still didn't sit well with him. "You really need to learn how to treat women better."

"I treat women just fine. I've never heard any complaints."

Chris decided not to have the usual argument. "I guess the plans for the weekend are off. I'll give you a call."

Evan nodded, his attention going back to the new bartender. As Chris left, he heard Evan sweet-talking her and knew he'd probably lose a bartender soon. Shaking his head, he walked back to the office, only to be waylaid by Lee. He gritted his teeth, trying to quash his rising irritation. There were a multitude of problems every night at Dupree's, from fighting busboys to drunk customers. But tonight, he didn't give a damn. He just wanted to get back to Cynthia.

"What do you need, Lee?"

Her eyes narrowed at his tone. Chris hadn't even tried to hide his annoyance with her.

"I just thought you'd like to know that I made sure we were covered tomorrow."

"I appreciate it. Is there anything else?"

"It seems that your—what is her name?—Cynthia is more important than your business."

Annoyance quickly transformed into anger, but he held on to it. They were within earshot of both the kitchen and a few tables. "Just a little information for you, Lee. I own Dupree's. It is *my* business, and I approve all hirings and firings. And a little advice—telling the boss what he should be doing, when you've only been here a month, isn't the way to go about getting a raise."

She opened her mouth to argue, but Maylea stopped her. "Lee, I think you're needed up front." Lee looked back over her shoulder at May. "And, so you can stop taking the credit, I was the one who made sure we had people here tonight and tomorrow."

Without another word, Lee tossed Chris a look of condescension, then marched off to go back to work.

"Ahh, *bra*," she said, using the familiar term Hawaiians used for close male friends or family members, "you'd better be careful with that one. She's gonna leave claw marks."

His smile dissolved into a frown. "What are you doing on your feet?"

She rolled her eyes and gestured to her sides. "I'm not on my feet. I am on crutches. There are other things of importance, like relieving oneself every now and then."

Chris laughed. "I guess we should chat about firing her."

"No, she's gonna quit. Mark my words. Girl is a waste of space, and now that she knows you're taken, *bra*, she won't care. This way, we won't have to pay unemployment."

"You're a cold-hearted woman, May." He leaned forward and brushed her cheek with a brotherly kiss. "I'm glad we never got involved."

A fine blush worked its way up her neck and into her face. "Chris, there was no way that could have happened."

"Why is that?"

"You remind me of my brothers. That's just...gross."

"Just remember, let someone else close up."

She nodded, but didn't meet his eyes.

"May..."

"I'll do it. Back off, *bra*." He stepped out of her way. After she passed, she paused and looked back over her shoulder. "Dennis took Cynthia something to eat a little while ago. Better watch out around her. The dogs are already sniffing."

He smiled as he watched her hobble back into the main dining area. May might be young, but she was smart and never failed to tell him exactly what she was thinking. It was at times refreshing and other times frustrating.

He headed back to his office and found the door slightly open. Muted voices drifted through the opening. May hadn't been wrong. He recognized Dennis's voice. One of the chefs, he was known for his string of tourist conquests. Jealousy, swift and unexpected, swept through Chris.

"So, one of the things you may not understand is how hard it is to concentrate in a commercial kitchen."

"Really?"

Chris chuckled. Her voice dripped with sugar, the type you used to kill someone too stupid to understand sarcasm.

"Yes. It takes a lot to focus on your duties."

"You don't say?" There was a sharper edge to her tone, and Chris worried Dennis might be out of his depth. Six weeks ago, he doubted Cynthia would have butchered someone verbally, but now...he wasn't so sure.

Just as he reached to push open the door, Dennis shoved his foot further in his mouth. "I know a woman with your background—"

"My background?" Cynthia's pitch had risen, a sure sign of agitation. He knew she'd taken pride in her work at Anna's shop. She wouldn't take kindly to Dennis telling her who she was.

"I can tell that you haven't really been introduced to our line of work. A lady such as yourself wouldn't understand what it takes."

Chris opened the door and decided to save his sous-chef from bodily harm. Cynthia was in his chair, practically breathing fire. Dennis sat on the corner of the desk, one arm resting on his leg.

"Dennis."

He jumped off the desk and faced Chris, his fair skin flushing. The tone in Chris's voice was enough to let Dennis know he'd overstepped his boundaries. The young man swallowed—hard.

"Chris. I was just—"

"Telling me what a wonderful place this is to work," Cynthia said as she popped out of her chair and walked around the opposite side of the desk. She smiled up at him and winked. Chris tried not to laugh, but it was too funny.

"I think you had a long enough break, Dennis."

Dennis nodded and walked out the door.

"It was nice to meet you, Dennis," Cynthia called after his retreating form. "That wasn't very nice of you," she chided Chris.

He grabbed her hand and pulled her closer, sliding his arm around her waist. "It was that or let you tear him a new one."

She gasped and looked up at him. Then she burst out laughing. She slipped her arms up his chest and behind his neck. "It was really hard to put up with his condescending tone."

"So, he's not your type?"

She wrinkled her nose. He dropped a kiss on the tip of it.

"I don't want a boy. What is he—twenty?"

"Twenty-one."

She sighed. "Well, my tastes are a bit different from little boys with red hair and more hormones than sense."

"Is that a fact?" He bent down and nipped at her lips.

"Hmm."

She leaned into his kiss, her mouth opening immediately. When he pulled back, he was happy to see the bemused look in her eyes. She licked her lips, and he groaned.

When she spoke, her Southern accent deepened. "I have to say, you are definitely catering to my tastes."

Hunger rose and every drop of moisture in his mouth evaporated. From the moment she'd stepped into his kitchen, he'd barely held onto his control by concentrating on the tasks at hand. Now that the time had finally arrived, one he'd dreamed of since she'd left that morning in Georgia, he couldn't be gracious. It was beyond him.

"I heard you had something to eat. Are you ready to leave?"

"Here's your hat, what's your hurry?" He opened his mouth, and she laughed. "I'm teasing. It has been a long day. It started early. My flight left about ten-thirty eastern time."

"What hotel are you staying at?"

"I'm not. That is what I wanted to talk about. I'm staying at my grandmother's old house."

"Why didn't you—?"

"I didn't tell you because I wasn't sure I'd have the nerve to stop by. Also, you've been so busy. I didn't want you to feel obligated."

"Well, it isn't an obligation, it's a need. Your grandmother lived in the North Shore area, right?"

She nodded.

"I'm closer. I live over in Hawaii Kai. Did you drive?"

"Yes, I rented a car until I can buy one. I'll follow you."

As he led her through the restaurant, Chris noticed Evan was now talking to Lee, and Maylea was sitting in her spot. The dinner crowd was dwindling, only a few hangers-on left at the bar. He stopped to talk to May. She didn't look like she was feeling well. Her shoulders were slumped, the circles under her eyes were pretty dark and she was frowning. She'd been in a wreck two days earlier, and she needed her rest. He knew she used work to escape her overbearing family.

"Why don't you go home, sista?"

She smiled, albeit weakly. "I will as soon as we lock up. I'm leaving all the cleaning up to everyone else." Turning her attention to Cynthia, she said, "It was really nice meeting you, Cynthia."

"Same here."

After a few more instructions, Chris led Cynthia out of the restaurant and into the cool night air. Moments later, she was following him in her rented convertible. As they neared his house, he began to worry. He had his plan—he would introduce her slowly to the D/s lifestyle—but what if he'd read her wrong?

He shook his head as he pulled into his driveway. No, this was right. He'd felt it almost from the first time he'd seen her, and whenever he heard her voice on the phone.

And tonight, he would start them both on the path to what he knew he needed and hoped she needed too.

Chapter Ten

Cynthia followed Chris up the steps to his house. He had a split-level, which was popular in Hawaii. It sat on top of a hill, the back of it facing the ocean. She concentrated on the surroundings, trying to ignore the pounding in her heart, the way her hormones were doing a tap dance, the way she had to keep from jumping his bones in public. Once he unlocked the door, he held it open and let her enter before him.

As she stepped across the threshold, her nerves ratcheted up another level. He hadn't touched her since they left Dupree's, but it didn't matter. She kept remembering what it felt like to have his hands...his mouth on her skin.

He flipped on a few lights, and she had her first real view of his house. The entryway led to a long hallway, which she assumed led to the bedrooms. The kitchen was off to the right. The floor, at least down the hallway, was tile, which she was sure kept the house cool. Her grandmother's was the same way. Familiar with the long-held Hawaiian tradition, Cynthia automatically removed her shoes. Chris arched a brow and followed suit. She smiled and shrugged.

"My grandmother insisted on following the traditions."

Placing his hand on the small of her back, he ushered her to the kitchen. It was an open area, with lots of counter space, that led into a living and dining area. She walked around until she came to the windows that looked out onto the lanai. Her breath caught in her throat as she gazed down on the twinkling lights of his neighborhood and out at the Pacific.

"I paid more than this house was worth at the time to get that view." He stepped behind her, sliding his arms around her waist and pulling her against him. "The house was a mess, but with Evan's help I got it just the way I wanted it." He rested his cheek on top of her head. "I need to take a shower. Why don't you relax, make yourself at home, and I'll be back in a minute."

He kissed her on the temple and left her alone to roam through his house. Okay, he hadn't said to roam, but he had told her to make herself at home. She wandered over to the bookshelves that lined two of his walls from floor to ceiling. The multitude of titles included works from Asimov to business books. On several of the shelves he had pictures of family members, all smiling, all with their arms around each other. Her family didn't have pictures like that. Odd, she'd never thought about it before, but the only pictures she had with her parents were done in a studio. Calm, staged, perfect. Not one of Chris's looked staged.

"I see you've met my gaggle of brothers and sisters."

She started and turned around. Chris stood a few feet behind her, droplets of water in his hair, only wearing a pair of black boxers.

Until this minute, she hadn't realized exactly how much she'd missed touching him. Her gaze roamed down his body and she sighed. She didn't know another man as beautiful as Chris. He moved, and she watched, mesmerized by the play of muscles beneath his skin. For once in her life, reality was better than memory.

"You keep staring at me like that, and I'm not going to be gentle."

She took her time shifting her attention back to his face. The tension in the room increased as she walked toward him. Stopping within a few inches of touching him, she closed her eyes and inhaled. The clean, woodsy scent of his soap mixed with his own unique scent. Heaven.

She opened her eyes. "Who asked you to be gentle?"

He smiled. "Now that is an interesting comment." He slid his arms around her waist and drew her against him. "I'd like to strip you naked and fuck you until sunrise."

She shivered. Usually—well, before Chris—remarks like that disgusted her. Now she just wanted to know if it were possible.

"There are things we need to talk about."

She worried at the serious tone in Chris's voice. It struck her as odd and threw her off center. From the moment she'd seen him in the kitchen, she'd known this was right. Now from his tone, she worried that maybe he'd felt obligated to bring her back to his home. Oh Lord. Just what she needed—pity.

Still, she couldn't keep her mind from wandering to thoughts of what she wanted him to do to her. She'd watched his lips as he talked, remembering the way they tasted, how they felt as he kissed his way down her body, slipped his tongue into her pussy.

"What kind of things?" And did it involve him naked?

"Not here." He pulled away from her and took her hand, leading her through the kitchen and to his bedroom. Once she stepped into the room, her body heated up about fifteen hundred degrees. An antique dresser sat against one wall, along with a rocking chair. On the opposite wall, his bed snagged her interest. King-sized, with a wrought-iron headboard, it was a high bed with a Hawaiian quilt covering it, green, red and blue interwoven through the pattern. Nightstands on each side of the bed matched the dresser. Both held identical lamps and provided the only light in the room.

"Why don't you have a seat?"

She hesitated and he cocked his head to the side.

"What's going on in that beautiful head of yours?" His voice had softened, his worry easy for her to hear. When she met his gaze, she tried to relax. Chris continued on, his voice softer, more understanding than before. "Don't get ahead of me. Just sit down and we'll work it out."

She nodded. All the delicious warmth that had been building now lay frozen. Doing his bidding, she settled onto the bed and concentrated on her bare feet.

He didn't say anything, but she felt his gaze on her. Slipping a finger under her chin, he lifted it. When she finally made eye contact, he continued.

"That night in Georgia..." He sighed. "This is really hard, so I'll just blurt it out. Did you feel like there was something different, something new about your experience with me that you didn't have with other men?"

Heat crawled up her neck and into her face. "Well, I told you...I hadn't been able to..."

"Did you ever wonder why?"

"I just thought you were very good."

He chuckled, and she smiled. "I am, but not *that* good. Let me put it another way. Did you ever feel that you didn't enjoy sex because...well, maybe you didn't feel as if you had a say in the action?"

"I wasn't raped."

He winced. "Okay, I'm not being as slick as I usually am. When you were telling me what to do, how did that make you feel?"

"I liked it." It was hard to admit, but the little play had turned her on.

"And would you like to do that again, have that play within the bedroom?"

She nodded, confused by his line of questioning.

He took another deep breath and swallowed. For some reason, his nervousness made her feel better, not so unsophisticated.

"I have a confession to make. I'm a switch. Do you know what that means?"

She shook her head.

"It means that I like to play both the role of dominant and submissive."

For a second her mind didn't compute the words, but then what he was saying hit the mark. "You're into S and M?"

"Not really. Well, a little. I'm more into bondage and submission."

Her mouth opened but she couldn't get her tongue to work. Her mind had frozen on the words *bondage and submission.*

"You like to tie women up—"

"Sometimes. Sometimes I like them to tie *me* up."

Her eyes widened at that comment. She couldn't say anything. Her head was still reeling with the ideas he had planted there. Most of all, a tide of hot lust rose up and almost overwhelmed her. She wasn't comfortable with the fact that the idea of tying him to the bed aroused her.

He shifted his feet restlessly. "Listen, what I like, and what you like—*that* is what's important. Cynthia, ask yourself, would you have been as fulfilled if you had not taken the lead that night and the next morning?"

The mention of their time brought back the experience in

vivid detail. She'd been a little pushy, and felt...powerful. She never would have associated that power with sex.

"I guess you're right, there."

He released a breath, as if he had been worried she'd deny it. "I'd like to help you feel that way...all the time."

She swallowed, wondering why the idea had her practically creaming. The image of Chris, tied to a bed, naked and at her mercy, had pleasure humming through her. Immediately, embarrassment and shame stole over her, telling her that this was not right, this was bad.

"No," Chris said, accurately interpreting the expression on her face. "Don't be ashamed of what you feel. It's healthy, and if you want, I'll try my best to teach you."

Fear and desire surged, twisting her inside out. Her upbringing was screaming at her, telling her this was wrong, that she was bad for wanting it. Somehow, she fought against those worries and looked him in the eye.

"I'm not promising anything, but...I want to try."

Chris's mind went blank. The woman he had been dreaming about for almost two months, been making plans for, was now saying she would try to learn what he wanted, and he couldn't form a sentence. Every ounce of blood must have drained straight to his cock, along with any working brain cells.

She was looking up at him with those cornflower-blue eyes, her lips painted red, his for the taking, and he couldn't think. Lust, almost too painful, coursed through him, but it also mixed with a dose of fear.

"Chris?"

The doubt in her voice pushed aside his worries. He shook his head, trying to pull out of his stupor, and smiled down at her. Holding his hand out, he waited for her to place hers in his, and then lifted her up off the bed.

"We won't do anything too demanding at first."

He moved behind her, never breaking contact. He trailed his hand up her arm to her shoulder. Her muscles tensed, though not out of fear—at least, he hoped not. He hoped it was out of anticipation. Breathing deeply, he massaged her shoulders, trying to ease her doubts. Taking it slow was going to drive him crazy. But he knew that this early in the relationship, he had to take measured steps. Someone who had never encountered the lifestyle might be overwhelmed by what they felt.

"Tonight will be about you. You tell me what to do with you...*to* you."

She drew in a shuddering breath, her muscles relaxing beneath his ministrations. "I'm not sure what to do, what to say."

Leaning closer, he brushed his lips against her ear and whispered, "Nothing between us is wrong. There is nothing to be embarrassed about, or shouldn't be. Pleasuring you, following your orders, is my duty. What I want to do."

"What if...?" She swallowed. He slipped his hands down her arms and tangled his fingers with hers. "What if I can't do it?"

Even as excited as he was, anger swirled within him. Damn her father and every man she'd ever been involved with before him for making her doubt herself like this, including Max. He tried to calm his temper by counting backward from ten. He didn't want her picking up on it, thinking it was directed toward her. When he spoke, he chose his words carefully.

"You do what you're comfortable with. You do what you want. There are no preconceived notions in this relationship."

"I don't know where to start, what to do."

"Well, you remember our night together."

He could hear the smile in her voice. "In Technicolor."

He chuckled. "Tell me what you liked about it."

As he waited for her answer, he moved his lips over the tender skin of her neck. He couldn't resist grabbing a taste of her, almost as if his life depended on it.

"I liked the way you made me feel."

"Go on." He switched to the other side of her neck, and she tilted her head to give him better access.

"I liked touching you."

"Hmmm." He didn't say anything else because he was gritting his teeth. She'd leaned back, and the fullness of her ass was pressed up against his dick. Every time she shifted her weight, he had to fight not to come then and there.

"There was a point..." Her voice trailed off as he nipped at her ear. "There was a point where you were sitting in the chair that morning after—well, and a little the night before—and for the first time, I was in charge."

Little did the woman know she'd probably been in charge since the moment she'd walked through the door in Georgia and smiled at him.

"How did that make you feel?"

"Powerful." She sighed. "I know it sounds crazy, but for some reason it aroused me more to tell you what to do."

Her excitement was growing. He could tell by the deepening of her voice, by the way her breathing had hitched as she told him her thoughts. Lord almighty, she was potent.

"So, you liked telling me what to do?"

She nodded.

"Why don't you tell me what you want now?"

She moved her hands to the hem of her shirt and tugged. He stopped her by placing his hands on hers, then turned her to face him. Surprise mixed with passion darkened her eyes.

"You let me do that. I'm the one here to serve, to make you happy."

The pulse in her neck jumped. "Yes." Barely a whisper, the husky sound of her voice washed over him.

As he reached for her, he realized his hands were shaking. It was amazing, considering his state of arousal, that he wasn't rolling around on the floor, babbling in tongues.

Slowly, inch by inch, he raised her shirt up over her torso until he finally revealed her bra. By the time he'd relieved her of the shirt, his heart was beating so hard, he was amazed he didn't pass out. He tossed her shirt behind him. Her bra was a far cry from the plain one she'd worn before. There was no fancy lace or designs, but the color grabbed his attention—fire-engine red, with one of those front hooks. Her ivory skin seemed almost translucent against the vivid color. Curling his fingers into his palms, he fought the urge to brush the backs of them over the swell of her breasts. The memory of circling his tongue around each nipple, remembering how her skin tasted...

Biting down on his frustration, he pushed himself to concentrate on Cynthia. Without taking his gaze off her, he asked, "What now? What would you like now?"

"My pants."

He was satisfied that her voice wasn't much steadier than his. He still couldn't look up. If her eyes reflected a smidgen of the lust he heard, he'd lose all rational thought. He'd strip her naked and slip his cock into her pussy before he had a chance to control himself.

After unsnapping her pants, he unzipped them, allowing the backs of his fingers to trail down her abdomen. The muscles quivered beneath his touch. He removed her pants, slowly sliding them down her legs. When he first saw the little matching panties, he about died. They barely covered her, and the sheer lace revealed more than it concealed. He could see right through them. The one thing he didn't see was hair.

As he stood, his cock brushed against her stomach. His balls twisted, his heart pounded, and he was thankful that she wasn't in the role of a true Domme. He was sure he'd embarrass himself if she were really in control.

Licking his lips, he asked, "What would you like now?"

She didn't say anything, but she captured his gaze, mischief sparkling in the depths of her eyes. Only inches separated them. She placed her hands on his chest. They were cool against his heated skin. Lightly, she moved them over him, her attention dropping from his face to her actions.

Her touch awakened something within him. It ignited an inferno that threatened to engulf him. She dipped one hand and glided it over his nipple. Curling his toes into the carpet, he watched as her lips quirked and she leaned forward. She replaced her hand with her mouth. Her tongue swiped over the nipple. A jolt of desire hit him fast and hard, his head spinning from the impact. He could smell her shampoo, the perfume that haunted his memories. When she finished tormenting that nipple, she kissed her way over to his other, giving it the same treatment.

By the time she was done, his breathing had deepened, his body was screaming for release, and all she had done was lick him. Without a word, she slipped her hands down his body to his boxers. She grabbed the waistband and pulled down, helping him step out of them and then tossing them aside. As she stood, her breasts brushed his shaft. The touch of her hardened nipples against his flesh caused a drop of cum to bead in the slit of his cockhead. He didn't know if her actions had been on purpose until he noticed her smug little grin.

"So, now you do what I want?" He could tell from her tone that her actions had aroused her as well. "Hmmm. Should it be something I want to have done to me? Or something I want to do to you?"

The playfulness in her voice sank beneath his skin, into his mind. She was getting into it, he could tell. He reminded himself not to rush, no matter how much he wanted to charge toward the finish line.

"That would be up to you. Whatever you want to do."

With a huff, she tilted her head to one side, stepped back and allowed her gaze to roam down his body. As she studied him, it was as if her hands were on him, traveling over his skin, driving him mad, pushing him closer to the edge.

"I think I need to catch up with you. I have too many clothes on. And then maybe we can work on just what you can do to make me happy."

The pulsing lust in his blood made it hard for him to do anything. But truth was, the way she talked, the way she was ordering him around, had him practically drooling. The woman might be a novice, but Lord help him, she knew how to push the right buttons.

He slowly unfastened the front closure of her bra, skimming his hands beneath the fabric to shift it aside. Brushing his thumb over a nipple, he smiled when she shivered. He cupped her breast while moving his other hand beneath the bra strap. Easing off first one strap and then the other, he allowed the bra to fall to the floor. He covered her other breast with his hand, enjoying the contrast in their skin tones. Even flushed with arousal, her skin was delicate ivory. Knowing the passionate woman who lurked inside added another delicious dimension to her.

By the time he touched her panties, both of them were breathing heavily. He slipped his fingers beneath the lacy waistband and skimmed those sinful red panties down her creamy thighs. He swept his fingers against the backs of her knees. When she almost lost her balance, he smiled. He continued to trail his fingers down her legs until he reached her ankles and helped her step out of the scrap of fabric.

She got up on the bed. Once she settled, he took a good, hard inspection of her body, noting the small changes. She had a few more curves that only added to her appeal. His gaze dropped to the apex of her thighs and confirmed his suspicions—she'd shaved her pussy bare. An extra pulse of heat twitched in his shaft, and he gave it one stroke, hoping to calm it a bit.

Her eyes narrowed at his action. "You're not starting without me, are you?"

The authority in her voice surprised him enough to drop his hands to his sides. She smiled at him.

As he stared down at her stretched out naked on his mattress, his heart stopped. She looked perfect, as if his bed had been waiting for her.

She patted the space beside her. "Come on, Chris."

He slid onto the mattress next to her. When he turned to take her into his arms, she shook her head.

"Hmm, I don't think so." She closed her eyes and rested against the stack of pillows behind her. "What I would like is for you to please me."

Okay, he didn't want to do that. Oh, he liked playing, but it had been too long, and frustration at the game—even though he had started it—made his tone rougher than usual.

"And how do you suggest I go about that?"

She frowned, but didn't open her eyes. "There's no need to get so upset. I'm not really sure what to do. I mean, how do I tell you how to do things?"

The worry in her voice brought him back to his senses. He needed to remember that for Cynthia, this was new. Chris imagined she would have never chosen this path before him. "Why don't I just start, and you tell me what you like, what you don't like, and we work from there?"

She caught her lip between her teeth and nodded.

Cautiously, he leaned forward and rasped his tongue over her nipple. He exhaled deeply and took the nipple into his mouth, sucking on it while he moved his hand up her body to her other breast. He rolled the nipple between his thumb and forefinger as he continued to work the first with his mouth. He teased both until they stood at attention.

He lifted his head and smiled. "So, what would you like for me to do now?"

Without opening her eyes, she took him by the back of the neck and pulled him down for a wet, almost-make-him-come kiss. Even as her tongue stole past his lips, she grabbed his hand and dragged it down to her pussy. Moist heat warmed his skin, and when he moved it against her, her juices dampened his hand.

She broke away from the kiss to emit a deep-throated moan that ran down his spine. "Use your fingers."

Wanting to push her further into her role, he teased, "But I am."

She opened her eyes slightly and frowned at him. "Slip them inside."

He did, without breaking eye contact, and was thrilled to

see her eyes go blank with passion, then slide shut as her muscles clamped down on his fingers. He continued his torment, and every so often he brushed against her clit. Soon, her hips were moving in rhythm with his fingers. He could tell from her movements that she was getting frustrated. A moment later, she opened her eyes and said, "I want your mouth on me."

"Hmmm." He pulled his fingers out, brushing against her clit one last time. He settled between her legs, his head above her belly. Kissing her navel, he smiled when the muscles quivered beneath his lips.

"Not there."

He glanced up and cocked an eyebrow, then leaned forward to kiss just below her bellybutton. "How about here?"

Her fingers grabbed the quilt. "No."

Moving an inch lower, he kissed her again, this time swiping his tongue against her skin. "Here?"

She growled, the sound of it music to his ears. The aggressiveness was new to her, and a step forward for both of them.

"No." Lifting herself to her elbows, she looked down at him. "I want your mouth on my...pussy."

There was no doubt in his mind—that had been an order. He ducked his head to hide the smile curving his lips. She might take it the wrong way. Pride marched hand in hand with desire. He lowered his mouth to just inches away from her. Taking a deep breath, he drank in the musky scent of her arousal. Anticipation skated along his nerve endings as he lowered his mouth and pressed it to her sex.

Sweet, hot, with a touch of spice, she tasted better than he remembered. His tongue dove between her drenched folds and then skimmed up to tease her clit. He continued this pattern, stealing inside, teasing that hard clit, until she moved her legs to rest on his shoulders. As he felt his own body responding more, his balls drawing up, his cock ready to explode, he slid his hands beneath her ass, lifting her closer. He couldn't get enough of her. Nothing had ever tasted as good as Cynthia.

He concentrated on her clit and slipped a finger inside of her. *Holy Jesus.* Her muscles contracted around him, and all he could think of was what it would feel like to thrust his cock back into that tight cunt.

Her moans increased, and her hands came to rest on his head, keeping him in place as he feasted. He increased the suction on her clit, and she came apart a moment later, her name on his lips as she convulsed.

"Oh, fuck yes, Chris!"

He lifted his head, but had little time to enjoy the view as she was already tugging him up her body. Without another thought, he obeyed, dragging himself up and over and entering her in one hard thrust.

Never before had it felt so right. Wet, pulsing, she surrounded him. He pushed himself up to his hands, her legs still draped over his shoulders, and began to move. Cynthia twisted her head from side to side as her pussy clamped down hard on his cock. He changed the angle of his thrusts and pushed her over the edge. As her muscles gripped his shaft, they pulled him into his own orgasm, his mind going blank to everything but pleasure.

Chapter Eleven

The next morning Cynthia sat at Chris's kitchen table reading over the paper, a cup of Kona coffee at her elbow. Chris was at the stove cooking pancakes he insisted on making her.

"So, what are your plans?"

She looked over at him and smiled. Wearing a pair of khaki shorts and an unbuttoned red Hawaiian shirt, he was a sight to watch as he worked around his kitchen. Last night had been beyond anything she could have imagined. He hadn't been satisfied with one bout, or two, she thought as she curled her toes against the cool tiled floor. Each time had been special. Sex with Chris was so different than what she'd experienced with her former lovers. She wasn't exactly sure why. It just was. She'd never felt so...in tune with a man before. It was odd since she had known Max most of her life. Here was a man she'd only met weeks earlier, but she sensed she knew him better than any man she'd been with. She may not be able to tell someone his favorite color, but she felt an intimacy with Chris she'd never achieved with Max.

"Cynthia?"

She shook her head and moved her attention back to his face. His smile told her that he understood exactly what she had been thinking. And still, she couldn't stop the blush that flushed her face.

"My plans? For today?"

He poured some batter on the griddle and nodded. "And beyond."

"Today, I need to go to my grandmother's house and start getting it in order. Then I thought I might just take a week or two and play tourist."

"Then back to Georgia?"

She shrugged, still worried he would take her decision the wrong way.

"How much time did you take off from work?"

"I quit."

He flipped one pancake over before doing the same with the second. "I thought you liked that job."

"I did, but I needed time to think, to sort things out. A lot of things happened in the last few weeks. I couldn't give Anna a definite date when I would be able to return."

He plated the food and set it on the table.

She frowned at the stack of pancakes in front of her knowing there was no way she would ever finish them. Before she could say anything, Chris said, "I'm cooking and you're my guest. Eat."

Chris poured more batter then refilled his coffee cup. "What kind of things happened?"

Cynthia didn't explain at first. It was more out of habit than anything else. So many years of not sharing family business was a hard trait to break. Chris glanced at her, a strange mixture of concern and hurt shading his expression. She didn't want him to think she was holding back.

"Family things." She picked up the syrup and poured a generous amount over her plate. Even with Max she'd rarely discussed family matters. Odd, seeing as he probably knew

140

more about her life than anyone else outside of the Myers' household. It had been drilled into her from birth not to share secrets, tell of their problems.

After cutting off a portion of pancake, she shoved it in her mouth. As she chewed, she watched Chris work the other pancakes, filling a second plate for himself. Strong, capable and unbelievably interested in her. Cynthia was sure those were the things that drew her to him, but there was more. Understanding, not pity, in his manner, in his expression made it easier to talk to him.

She cleaned off the remnants of the syrup from her mouth and drew in a cleansing breath. "There seemed to be a part of my grandmother's will that my father neglected to tell me about."

And so she told him. Over coffee and pancakes, the whole sordid story gushed out of her. From finding out about her father's financial problems, to the news that he had planned on stealing from her, to the final nasty confrontation with her mother the night before she drove to Atlanta. Instead of being disgusted with her because of her family, he was incensed on her behalf.

"Did you go to the police about it?"

She sighed. "No. Truthfully, he hadn't actually committed a crime. I could have set him up, allowed him to take over and then have him arrested. In fact, my lawyer wanted to do just that. He was most insistent that I do."

"I'd like to buy him a drink."

Smiling, she watched as he poured her another cup of coffee. "I just wanted it over. If there had been a trial—because I know my father would never admit to anything—I would have been stuck in Georgia for who knows how long. It's better this way."

"Better that you're here with me even if I would like to beat your father to a pulp."

He said it with such a calm tone that she laughed. "I think my grandmother would have liked you."

"Really? I've never been a man grandmas like. Well, except my own."

"My grandmother was a bit of a progressive, especially for coming from such an old Southern family. She believed in free love, and she definitely believed in following your heart. I know, although my parents tried to hide it from me, that she was living with her boyfriend when she died."

"Nothing wrong with that."

"No, but then, he was half Hawaiian and half black. Not the thing to do, according to my father. Besides, she hated my father."

"Then I think I would have very much liked your grandmother." He reached across the table, took her hand in his, tangling their fingers. "Feel better?"

"Yes." The weight she had been bearing seemed to be lifting. She wasn't used to having someone to share her worries with. "Thanks for listening."

"No problem. So, back to your visit." He caressed the delicate skin between her thumb and index finger, his concentration on their joined hands. The intensity of his gaze caused her heartbeat to accelerate.

"I'm not visiting."

He paused and looked at her. "What are you saying?"

She drew in a deep breath and said, "I'm seriously thinking about moving here."

Chris studied her for a couple of seconds, his expression completely blank. His lips curved. "I like that idea." He stood, tugging her up out of her chair. "How about I show you how much I like it."

☯

Chris settled against the pillows in his bed while he watched Cynthia pull on her pants. He sighed with regret when her red panties disappeared from view. It was a shame he was still naked, ready for another bout of lovemaking, and she was getting dressed.

"I thought if some of my crew actually showed up not sick today we could go out tonight."

She glanced at him and smiled. The sight of it hit him right in the chest, his heart flip-flopping. He couldn't believe she was here.

"I think that is a great idea. I have to head on over to my grandmother's house, get the things taken care of. I need to check to see if any mail has arrived and make sure they start delivering to the house."

She tugged her shirt over her head, then ran her hand through her hair. The sleek bob she'd had when he met her was now a mass of golden curls. The changes in her appearance and in her demeanor were amazing. The reserve she'd used to shield herself was still there, but beneath the surface he sensed her acceptance that she was someone other than that buttoned-down, unhappy woman.

"How about I take you out on the town, show you Waikiki and Honolulu nightlife."

"I'd like that a lot."

She placed her hands on the bed and leaned close, her lips brushing over his. It was barely a touch, not much of a kiss, but the sweet, hot taste of her had his blood humming and his cock stirring. Not able to resist, he slipped his hand up over her shoulder to the base of her neck. He tangled his fingers in her silky mane, adding pressure to the back of her head, urging her to deepen the kiss. When she complied, he groaned and yanked her down on top of him, then rolled over, reversing their positions.

By the time he pulled back from the kiss they were both breathing heavily, and a pretty flush of heat colored her chest and face.

"Chris, I need to get some things done today."

He loved the way she talked, especially when she was aroused. Southern hospitality with a douse of sin warmed that chilly Junior League tone.

"But just one more little meal will keep the beast at bay for a few hours."

She opened her mouth to argue and he leaned down to kiss her again, stopping any opposition. As usual, she returned his ardor, causing another pulse of lust to shoot through his blood.

He dipped down, nipping and licking her jaw, then throat. Through the fabric of her shirt he kissed each breast but continued his descent to his target. It didn't take much to convince her to take off her pants and panties. The lips of her pussy were already dewy with desire. Chris drew in a deep breath, taking in the musky scent of her passion, enjoying that he could make her this hot this fast.

Wanting—no needing—a taste, he slipped his tongue into her slit and moaned. Soon, she was coming, her body bowed with her orgasm. Chris slid up her body and drove into warm, wet cunt. As he moved, he felt her building to another peak, and this time he wanted to be with her. Moments later, they came, her fingernails digging into his shoulders as he shouted her name.

He collapsed on top of her, and when she grunted from the blow of his weight, he rolled to his side. His breath caught at the sight of her pleasure. Her eyes were closed, her skin flushed, and she wore a cat-ate-the-canary smile. The hair she had been trying to tame earlier was in disarray again.

Chris didn't think he'd ever get enough of her. Did she know how she affected him? How with each little sigh she was killing him by inches? The need to tell her of his feelings, to tell her he loved her, almost overwhelmed him, but he knew she wasn't ready. If he proclaimed it now, she wouldn't believe him, and worse, she would run. He couldn't have that.

Chris leaned down to kiss her temple and smiled as she snuggled closer to him. He just hoped it wouldn't take much more to convince her of it because he didn't know how long he could hold back the words.

Cynthia juggled the load of mail she'd picked up at the PO as she tried to get her front door unlocked. She almost dropped all of it when her cell phone played Beethoven's Fifth, heralding a call from Max. It took a couple more tries before she got the key in the lock. When she pushed it open, she stumbled across the threshold, her mail falling from her arms, scattering across the wooden floor. The cell had quit ringing but just as she figured it would, it started up again. Max never could wait for voice mail.

She pulled the phone out of her pocket and clicked it on.

"I just left yesterday," she said without greeting him hello.

"Maybe I miss you."

She snorted and bent to pick up the letters. "Yeah, right. What do you want?"

"Anna wanted me to check and make sure you're getting settled in."

She paused in her retrieval of a credit card bill. "What happened?"

"What do you mean?"

"Max, Anna wouldn't tell you to call, she'd call herself. Something else happened."

He sighed, the sound of it filled with regret. "Georgia Bureau of Investigation announced that your father is under investigation."

She sat on the arm of an overstuffed sofa, her mind going blank. When it started working again, she asked, "What for?"

Max didn't say anything for a second or two. Knowing her father it could be anything.

"Bribery of a state official. It has something to do with a project for the University of Georgia."

She closed her eyes as regret and pain lanced through her. Her father was a horrible parent, but she didn't want something like this to happen to him. "Seriously, Max, do you think they have anything?"

Again, he paused and worry morphed into panic. "You know your father."

"Yeah, so it's a definite possibility." She tossed the envelopes onto the coffee table and rubbed her temple, trying to ease away the headache threatening to explode. "Do you think this is why he was trying to steal my money?"

Maybe he had been worried about his defense, of going to jail. It was almost understandable in a sick kind of way. Of course, Max broke through those illusions.

"No. I have a feeling your father had no idea this was coming. Apparently the investigation has been kept under wraps. Stealing your money was just more convenient than having to live up to the fact that he is, or pretty close to, bankrupt." When she didn't say anything, he continued. "Your father has some heavy mortgages on almost all his properties."

"I know." She hated the way her voice sounded, like a little girl unsure of what to do. She hated that her damn family was ruining her first full day in Hawaii. Truly, it was petty of her to think of herself considering what the rest of the family was going through, but, dammit, she hadn't been the one who bribed an official.

"I don't want you feeling guilty about this."

She smiled. "How did you know?"

"I heard it in your voice, and I know you well enough to know you would. You have no reason to feel that way. Your father has been getting away with a lot for a long time. And you will *not* send him money."

She ignored the last comment completely. "If you don't want me to feel guilty, why did you call to tell me?"

"I figured you would find out soon enough, and I wanted you to hear it from a friend."

Her heart warmed. It had been a long few months since their breakup as she faced the disapproval of her family and pity from her acquaintances, but she had gotten two very precious friends out of the bargain. In her mind, it had made it worth it.

"Thanks, Max."

He cleared his throat the way he always did when he was embarrassed. "So, how is everything there? Have you been out yet?"

Cynthia chuckled, knowing exactly what Max was asking. "Everything is fine. I just got in from the post office. I stopped there after seeing Chris."

"So you went out to see him this morning?"

She laughed at that. "You don't play subtle when you act like my big brother."

"Cynthia..."

"Listen, what I do with and to Chris is my own business. He's one of your best friends, and I can't see why you would have objections to it, but if you do, too bad."

"There are things about Chris you don't know."

"I doubt that. But if you are talking about certain aspects of his personal life, well, again, none of your business. For the record, I already know about that."

"Cynthia—"

"Let it go. I'm a big girl and I can take care of myself."

"All right. I'll let it go, but remember, Anna and I are here for you."

"Thanks," she said with feeling.

Again, he cleared his throat. "Now, tell me about your plans."

Chapter Twelve

Two weeks after getting to Hawaii, the need to work was getting under Cynthia's skin. As she sipped at her Lava Flow, she looked out over Honolulu Harbor and watched the sun set. Chris was running late, mainly because Lee was late for her shift again. Not wanting to wait, she'd grabbed one of the Bubba Gump waiters and ordered her preferred drink since arriving on the island. Now, she was staring out over one of her favorite locations thinking that she had been waiting too long to begin the rest of her life.

Her relationship with Chris seemed to be moving along, but the restlessness that had started a week ago was now taking over most of her thoughts. It surprised her how much she missed working at Anna's restaurant. Of course, a lot of it was the companionship of the customers and her coworkers there, but a part of her missed the regular duties that had filled her day.

If someone had told her six months earlier that she'd miss getting out of bed at four in the morning, she'd have called them insane. Who would have thought she'd yearn to spend her mornings up to her elbows in dough? She'd lived a life of privilege. In high school, she'd put out feelers with her parents about working. Both of them denied her the right. She hated feeling useless and had for so many years. That all stopped when Anna had hired her. That job had given her a purpose in life, something she could be proud of. It proved that she was worth more than a marriage to further the family's interests.

"Sorry I'm late," Chris said, interrupting her thoughts. In a gesture she had come to expect and love, he leaned down and gave her a quick, hard kiss before taking the seat opposite her. "Lauren called to complain about Mamma and I had to wait for Lee. I have a feeling that woman isn't going to be late again for awhile."

She smiled at him and had to fight the urge to pinch herself to prove that she was really there with him. He was dressed casually, as usual, but was just as delectable in the loose white cotton shirt and jeans as he was the first time she had seen him dressed in a suit. Of course, she preferred him wearing nothing at all.

"Did you lay into her finally?"

Before he could answer her, the waiter stopped to ask for Chris's drink order. Once they were alone he smiled at her. "No, but May did. That girl can be ruthless when it comes to showing up on time." He shook his head. "So many people underestimate her because of her age and because she has a soft heart."

"Not you."

He reached across the table and took her hand in his. This was another gesture she'd gotten used to. Well, almost. She'd never thought of herself as overly demonstrative. Her family shunned displays of affection...even in private. The simple act of hand-holding was more than she ever got from her parents. Even now, surrounded by a rowdy crowd of tourists on a Friday night, heat scorched her blood. The familiar tide of lust slowly wound its way through her. Tenderness from Chris had the ability to make her want to jump his bones right there in the middle of the restaurant.

"No. Not me. I knew from the time I hired her when she was still in high school that she would make a fantastic manager. She's been spending enough time herding that group of men she lives with, little catty waitresses are child's play to her."

May lived with her grandfather, father and several of her brothers. Cynthia had yet to learn the whole story, but Chris had told her that May's mother died when May was a teenager.

"Hmm, so Lee still has a job?"

He nodded and then thanked the waiter for his drink. "Yeah, but probably not for long. May doesn't have much patience for her. And then there's the problem with Evan."

"Evan?"

"Apparently he's dating Lee and I tend to lose my staff when he does that."

Cynthia frowned, thinking of Chris's friend. She liked him well enough but something about Evan made her uncomfortable. It wasn't uncommon for her to act reserved when she first met someone. With Evan it was different. He wore charm as a shield, using it to keep people from looking too closely at the man beneath. It was that man who worried her. "Why are you friends with him?"

Chris didn't answer right away, as if carefully choosing his response. "When I was heavy into the BDSM scene, I wasn't always accepted. Many see a switch as unacceptable, not a true player. Evan always accepted who I was and what I was. Even being a true Dom like he is, he had no problem with me."

"Still, I just don't see you two as friends. Well, I do, but it is odd. Max seems more like you."

"No, you think that because you're comfortable with Max. Our view about life is very different." He took a sip of his drink.

"I'd like for you to get to know Evan better."

She frowned. "Why? I mean, I don't mind talking to him, but—"

His burst of laughter stopped her. "Lord, you're sexy when you put on that lady-of-the-manor attitude."

"What do you mean by that?"

"That tone." His tongue darted out over his bottom lip. Anticipation hummed between them. "It turns me on."

"It does?"

"Yeah, 'cause I know exactly how hot you can get. I know what you sound like when you moan."

His voice dipped into that New Orleans accent she loved. It slithered down her spine, brushed over her nerve endings. But she wouldn't be deterred.

"Stop that."

The grin he offered told her he knew exactly what he was doing to her.

She wasn't going to let him change the subject. "I just wondered how you two became friends since you're so different."

"Opposites attract?" He shrugged. "Odd, but true, especially friends. You may think Max and I are alike, but we aren't, not in our personal tastes. Same with Evan. But all three of us are accepting of other people, of their choices in life. For Evan, I think it comes from his childhood. There are things, things from his past, that explain his behavior."

She really wanted to know what those things were but knew better than to ask. Chris would never reveal those secrets, not without Evan's permission.

The waiter interrupted them once more for their food orders. Once he left, Chris said, "I can't believe you made me come to a rival for dinner."

She chuckled. "Count it as a busman's holiday. Besides"—she gestured toward the opened window—"I love the view."

He followed her direction and smiled. "I have to agree with you there."

Neither of them said anything for a bit, just taking in the sight of the sun sinking below the horizon, the boats bobbing in the Honolulu Marina.

"I'm thinking of opening a bakery." She didn't look at him, but she sensed his focus was now completely on her.

"Here in Honolulu?"

"Or up on the North Shore. I thought I'd look around for a shop that was reasonably priced."

He didn't say anything, so she gathered her courage and glanced across the table at him. "What do you think?"

"Hmm. I think that it's hard to start a business, especially in the food industry."

She pursed her lips and tried to fight back the wave of disappointment that swept through her. Cynthia had been so sure of his support.

"Oh, don't look like that. I just wanted you to think about what you're getting into. It isn't easy." When she didn't say anything, he tugged on her hand. "Stop thinking I'm going to condemn you for every thought. I happen to think it's an excellent idea."

"Really?"

He smiled. "Yeah, with your talent, you could probably do very well."

The excitement that gripped her every time she thought about opening her own bakery bounced back to life. "I wasn't thinking of anything big. Just a little shop, something in a good location with a lot of morning traffic."

"I have a great real estate agent who can help you scout locations. He's excellent with negotiations and if you find a place in need of some renovations, I'll blackmail Evan to help."

She bit her lip, trying her best not to let her emotions bubble over and embarrass both of them. No one, other than Anna, had ever pushed her, believed in her ability. To have the one man who meant the most to her encourage her, well, it was almost too much. He squeezed her hand. The simple gesture reassured and calmed her. It was as though he knew exactly what she needed.

"Thanks, Chris."

"It's no problem."

She couldn't allow him to dismiss it so easily, as if it meant nothing. "No, it isn't, but thank you for the support."

He said nothing for a second, then reached across the table to give her a long, slow, sweet kiss. "Anything for you, love," he whispered against her lips. She leaned into the kiss, slipping her tongue between his lips and taking his face into her hands.

Someone cleared their throat, breaking into the private moment, and Chris pulled back. The waiter had returned with their salads. Instead of the normal embarrassment that usually held her tongue-tied in these types of situations—not that she had been caught kissing a man in the middle of a restaurant on a regular basis—she just smiled at the young man while he did his duty.

"That was a first."

"Just wait." He wiggled his eyebrows. "Before long you'll be a regular wild woman."

She laughed and thought that it sounded like a good thing to be.

Several weeks later, Chris was busy trying to finish off a day's work to get to his wild woman. He closed his eyes and massaged his temples. The throb that had been there most of the day refused to go away. Even the pain reliever he'd taken hadn't eased a bit of the pain. A surprise health inspection, troubles with scheduling conflicts with some of the waitstaff's new school schedules, his mother's concern over some problems with his sister Jocelyn, and May informed him money was missing.

Opening his eyes, he looked at his computer. The screen showed the proof that someone on staff had been skimming a dollar here and there...at first. In the last few weeks, the amount had grown, causing May to notice it in the books. Anger and disappointment burned in his gut. He hated to think one of his own was stealing from him.

The knock at the door interrupted his depressing thoughts.

"Come."

The door opened and May poked her head in. "Ready?"

He nodded, the weariness of the day weighing heavy on his mind. She slipped through the doorway and sat in front of him.

"I did some research. Seems that every night we lost money, Lee was working."

"And?"

"She has to be the one."

He studied the young woman for a second. May's feelings about Evan and Lee dating were known to him. The attraction she had for Evan was hard for most people to miss. That was one of the reasons Chris was sure Lee went after Evan. She'd hated dealing with May from the beginning of her employment.

"I know what you're thinking, boss, and you're wrong."

"Prove me wrong."

She rose and came around the desk, handing him some papers with schedules and payroll on it. "I went back through all days we lost money. You know at first it wasn't much, one reason neither of us caught it. But then here"—she pointed at the computer screen, indicating the date two weeks ago that a little over a hundred dollars went missing—"is where she started getting careless."

"I know that. But how do you know it was her and not just someone else who worked those days?"

"She was the only one who worked every one of those days, Chris. No one else was scheduled and clocked in those days the money went missing. Not every single day."

He looked over the papers she handed him, then up at the screen where the days the money went missing were highlighted. "Hell."

"Yeah."

He glanced up at her, surprised to see the look of regret on her face. "What?"

"The fact that I found the information isn't going to sit well, and it will have a lot of people talking."

"I don't think you need to worry about that. Besides, you aren't firing her. I am."

Her shoulders sagged with what appeared to be relief. She leaned down and brushed her lips over his cheek. "Thanks, bra."

"Just remember you owe me one."

She headed to the door, but paused and turned to face him. The seriousness shimmering in the depths of her

Caribbean blue eyes stunned him. He often forgot just how young she was because she took on so much responsibility. "I appreciate you listening to me, Chris. Most employers wouldn't, considering."

He nodded, not saying what they both knew. She was infatuated with Evan, or had been, and a lot of other people might assume she zeroed in on Lee because of her crush. Chris knew better. No matter what her personal feelings were, May was a professional, through and through.

"Send Lee back when you go out there."

When she left him, he mentally prepared himself to fire Lee as fast as possible so he could get home to Cynthia.

By the time Chris pulled up to his house, most of his anger was just a memory. A little still burned his gut, along with a healthy dose of worry. Lee had not been easy to get rid of. Before she left, she made accusations that would never hold weight, but could hurt both Dupree's and May. Things about him, things that weren't true, but that didn't matter. If she filed charges of sexual harassment, it would hurt him in the business community. She'd never win in court because everyone who worked there knew of her pursuit of him—and knew he turned her down. But the attention would not be good and May didn't need more stress in her life.

He turned off his car and stepped out of it. Just being here, knowing Cynthia was waiting for him, caused his body to relax. The stress of the day dissolved with the anticipation of seeing her.

As he walked up the steps to his front door, he thought of

the last couple of weeks and the changes in Cynthia. She was gaining more confidence every day. When he'd talked to her earlier, she'd been reading her favorite book of late, *Sensuous Magic.* Chris had suggested the classic BDSM guide.

More than once he'd felt something else simmering beneath her surface, a hunger she wasn't fulfilling. Chris knew better than to push or prod. Cynthia needed to take the steps in her development without feeling forced and one of those steps was to take complete control of the situation. He sensed her desire for it, wanting to command his every action, but she didn't feel ready to take that last step. Knowing he had to wait until she understood her true Domme personality before he could take her under his control was driving him out of his ever-loving mind. Each step she took pushed him a little closer to the edge of sanity. He could feel it slipping from his fingers.

When he reached the top of the stairs, the door opened. Cynthia moved into view, an understanding smile lighting her face.

"May called."

He nodded but said nothing as he slid his arms around her body and pulled her close to him. The warmth of her, her unique scent, wrapped around him, draining the rest of the irritation from the day. Even the simple touch had his body reacting. His cock hardened as he leaned into her.

She hummed at the contact then nipped at the sensitive flesh just beneath his earlobe. He shuddered. She skimmed her fingers down his back, allowing him to feel the bite of her nails through his cotton dress shirt. Cupping his ass with one hand, she squeezed. His dick jerked in response, eager for the same attention.

"Let's get inside before I strip you naked and jump your bones with Mrs. Fukisamo looking on." Her breath was warm against his skin when she spoke.

He released her with a grunt. Cynthia threaded her fingers with his and led him into the house. Gladly, he followed her, wanting nothing more than to fall into her arms and into bed.

They dined on the lanai, watching the sun set on the horizon. He didn't often get dinner at home, only one or two a week. Owning a restaurant made it hard to break away, so he truly treasured these times. The light supper of Caesar salad topped with grilled salmon was just the right thing. As they chatted about mundane things—her day, his, the new recipe she found—a rightness warmed his heart. Chris wanted to demand that she accept him, and the kind of relationship he wanted for the two of them. That she see how perfect this was— and could be. But he kept those things locked inside of him, waiting for the cue from her that she was ready.

The easygoing feeling of the evening drifted away as they finished the dishes and she led him to the bedroom. Tension crackled between them. His blood hummed through his veins, his hunger for her growing with each step.

They entered the bedroom where she had set the stage for their evening of pleasure. Cynthia had taken time to place candles around the room, beside the bed, on his dresser, in various places. She released his hand and picked up a lighter.

With careful movements, she went from candle to candle, lighting each. There was no sound but the rustle of her clothing and his breathing. Anticipation had his pulse escalating, but he waited. He understood they were taking another step in their relationship. On every level—sexual and emotional—she'd methodically taken more power. It was her decision on what came next.

She turned to face him, her features cast in the wavering shadows produced by the candlelight. Her gaze raked over him as she sank onto a bench he had placed beneath the window.

Her lips curved when she asked, "Is there a reason why you're still clothed?"

Chapter Thirteen

Cynthia drew in a deep breath as she watched Chris. No matter how many times she'd seen him without clothes, it still made her heart skip the moment she was granted the privilege. Cream coated her pussy lips and the pressure between her legs intensified. She'd been thinking about this all day, planning this for most of a week, and now that it was actually happening, she'd be amazed if she could contain her eagerness.

The need to assert more control had built over the last few weeks, with each day, each time they made love. The research she'd done had given her confidence to attempt this action. A big step, yes, but one of many she had left to take.

Even so, her palms dampened, a slight chill slinked down her spine.

So she was nervous, of course she was. Who the hell wouldn't be nervous about telling a six foot god of a man to strip for her pleasure? Although at the moment, she was losing a bit of the conviction she had gained. Trepidation snuck into her mind. She shook it away, ignoring any of the negative thoughts that might pop up. This next step was natural and exactly what both of them needed.

He pulled the black cotton shirt out of his pants then slid each button free. As soon he'd undone the last one, he slipped it off. Knowing the game, he folded the shirt and put it on the occasional chair that sat next to the door. His hands trembled as they went to the waist of his pants. It was hard not to notice that or the long, hard ridge of his erection easily seen against the soft fabric of his trousers. Seeing his excitement spurred her own, but she tried her best to mask it. It took him two attempts to unfasten the button at the top then unzip his pants. To her disappointment, red cotton instead of skin appeared behind the zipper. The knit boxers were a favorite of hers but she'd hoped for nothing. The snug fit afforded her a wonderful view of his cock. As he turned to place his pants with his shirt on the chair, she couldn't stop herself from leaning to the side to get a better view of his rounded ass.

When he straightened again, his lips quirked.

"Something you find amusing?" she asked, proud that she'd kept her voice so cool while her body almost went up in flames.

"No. It pleases me to please you."

Without any other explanation, he slipped his fingers beneath the band of his shorts and tugged them down. The motion of removing them didn't allow for her to see his shaft. He didn't rush. With slow, measured movements, he skimmed the fabric down his legs. He took his time, drawing out his action, heightening their excitement. When he'd placed them with the rest of his clothes, he turned to her. His erect penis curved up to his belly.

"Spread your legs."

He obeyed and she stifled a moan. Her greedy gaze roamed over him, zeroing in on his cleanly shaved testicles. Every drop of moisture in her mouth evaporated as she fought the urge to place her lips there. To nip with her teeth and pull the sensitive skin into her mouth to suckle.

All in good time, Cynthia.

She rose to her feet. Her juices had flowed so freely, the tops of her thighs were wet. With each step she took, she reached a new level of tension. The friction caused her to wince. As she approached him his nostrils flared as if trying to scent her. Her nipples tightened in reaction. The action spoke of a basic need, primal desire.

She stepped behind him. With a featherlight touch, she skimmed her fingers over his ass, enjoying the way it clenched in reaction. Dipping one finger in the crevice between his cheeks, she smiled when he shifted his weight from foot to foot. She bent forward, placing her open mouth on his shoulder blade, and slipped her hand down to caress his sac. A surprised indrawn breath told her he hadn't expected that. She continued to move her mouth down his back as she massaged his testicles. His flesh was dewy with perspiration, the sweet, salty taste of it filling her senses.

She dropped to her knees, replacing her fingers with her mouth and taking his cock in her hand. As she sucked and licked him, Cynthia caressed his sex. Each time her hand stroked up, she rubbed her thumb over the tip. His breathing increased as he muttered. She increased her rhythm, driving him to the brink. Another drop of precum wet her fingers, and just as she sensed he was ready to let loose, she pulled away. Aggravation filled his groan.

"I didn't say you could come yet, Chris."

Knowing anticipation made the release she would give him even sweeter, she stood and walked around his body, tracing her fingers over his flesh. When she stepped in front of him, she stood so close she brushed his erection.

Reaching out with her finger, she circled the top of his cockhead, smiling when it twitched. She tilted her head back, nipping at his chin. "Now. You've been pretty good." Wrapping her hand around his cock, she pumped it twice. "I think you deserve a bit of a reward. One that I'll enjoy."

She lowered herself to her knees in front of him. "I'm going to suck you until you come."

He looked down on her, his defiance easy to see in his features and glittering in his eyes. He enjoyed the act, actually loved getting head. But Cynthia knew he wanted to hold out his enjoyment as long as possible.

"No. You will do this because I want to give it to you." She pronounced each word precisely as excitement gripped her chest. Her nipples beaded further, almost painful now. Her cunt pulsed at the thought of her plans, of controlling him until his orgasm.

Without another word, she leaned forward and took him into her mouth. As she worked him in and out, her hand followed along. She stroked his balls, squeezing them, then raked her nails over them.

"Cynthia." He moaned her name as if it were a plea. "Baby—"

She slipped her mouth over the entire length of him, cutting off whatever he was going to say. Closing her eyes, she continued deep throating him, pushing him, wanting him to lose all control. His moans grew loader, his fingers threaded into her hair. As she caressed his sac one last time, she drew him in.

"Cynthia!"

He pumped his hips as his seed shot to the back of her throat. Cynthia didn't stop her movements, continuing the rhythm until he stilled his hips.

With one last loving lick, she pulled him out of her mouth and looked up at him. The intensity in his eyes filled her with a combination of pride and tenderness. He opened his mouth, but

164

nothing came out. It was the first time she had pushed him this far, that she had completely controlled his orgasm. This had been about her control, her domination of him. From his behavior to his reaction, Chris had shown her that he understood just what it had been about.

She rose to her feet, took his hand and led him to the bed. Quickly, she rid herself of her clothes, then joined him under the covers. Arousal still hummed, her sex still ached with need, but she knew it was more. The heightened excitement came from his pleasure, from his enjoyment of allowing her to make him come.

He wrapped his arms around her and brushed his lips over her forehead. "I haven't taken care of you."

She smiled against his skin. "Don't you worry. You will. Let's just rest here for a second."

Pleased with the results of all her hard work, Cynthia let her thoughts drift. They'd turned a corner tonight. It was now her game, hers to control. She still had a ways to go in her sexual development, but now that she had reached this point, there was no going back.

A slight breeze lifted Cynthia's fair hair as she sipped her water and read the menu of a popular barbeque restaurant. The changes in her during the last month amazed Evan. No one would argue that she'd been attractive when she arrived. He'd always had a soft spot for Southern women. The slow, easy way their accent wrapped around words, as if savoring each one, drove him insane. How any man could be in a Southern belle's presence and not think of lazy mornings in bed was beyond him. He might have even tried her on for size, but he didn't

165

poach—at least not from Chris.

"What's good here?" she asked, pulling him out of his thoughts.

"Their Carolina Barbeque is good. If you like pork."

She glanced at him and smiled. "I'm a Southern girl at heart so of course I like pork. I think it's a requirement."

"That and sweet tea."

She set down the menu. "Where are you from originally?"

Out of habit, his defenses rose up before he could stop them. Even something as simple as telling a person where he'd grown up brought back the memories he'd rather forget.

"South Carolina. Florenceville, mainly."

She studied him for a second, then nodded. Taking a deep breath, she opened her mouth to respond, but the waitress came over for their orders. After the young woman left, Cynthia turned her attention back to him.

"I have some family on my mama's side up in that area. Do you know any of the Shipleys?"

Everyone did. One of the richest families in town, they employed a good portion of the working class, in their businesses and their homes. Hell, his mother had earned a living cleaning the home of one of them. Before the drugs. Before the nightmare that became their lives. The darkness of his childhood pressed in on him. His chest contracted, his lungs seized. Sweat dampened his palms. Taking a moment, he mentally counted back from ten but it did no good. Anger sharpened his voice when he answered. "No, not really."

Apparently picking up on his tone, she changed the subject. "How did you and Chris meet?"

Still irritated, he asked, "Just what the hell do you want, Cynthia?"

Her eyes widened at the question. Cocking her head to one side, she studied him as if he were some kind of animal in the zoo. Other memories of dingy offices, overworked city employees, and the all-too-uncomfortable questions rushed at him so fast he couldn't stop them.

"I thought we were supposed to get to know each other. Chris wants us to be at least friendly, if not friends."

She didn't know his past. Chris would never reveal that information without Evan's permission. It wasn't Cynthia's fault that her innocent questions brought those things back up. He smiled to cover his mood.

"There is that. I think I'd like to be friendly with you."

The waitress returned with their drinks. After she left, he continued. "I know we're both doing this for Chris, but I wondered why you aren't comfortable around me."

Her eyes narrowed and fire snapped within the blue. His body reacted to the look, the anger that simmered beneath the cool Southern veneer. Damn but she would be a wildcat to break.

"What did Chris tell you?"

He held his hands up. "Hey, take it easy. Chris didn't tell me anything. I swear."

She crossed her arms beneath her breasts and frowned at him. He couldn't help but notice the rounded flesh that rose above the neckline of her sweater. "Why don't you think I like you?"

He settled his hands on the table. "I didn't say that. I said you weren't comfortable. But, now that you said it, I think we should discuss why you don't like me."

"I didn't say I didn't..." She huffed out an annoyed sigh, then made a face. "Okay, part of me doesn't like you. Or at least the part of you the world gets to see."

Again, she was too close for comfort and he didn't like it one damn bit. "Are you saying that I'm hiding something?"

She shrugged. The dainty gesture drew attention to the smooth skin on her shoulders. The ruby red sleeveless sweater she wore enhanced the tan she'd gotten in the last six weeks. The bit of color had added warmness to her features and accentuated the thin line of gold that rimmed those blue eyes. Humidity had taken control of her hair, causing it to curl. The multitude of highlights from the sun now wove through her heavy locks. Need slipped under his skin, and he suddenly found himself ravenous. He craved to slide his hands into her mane as she closed that wicked mouth over his cock. Evan would love to return the favor and find out just how closely the curls between her legs matched the hair on her head.

"You just don't seem to want anyone to know what you're really like."

Her voice broke into his fantasy and the desire that had surged died almost instantly. She was right. There was only one person who knew about Evan's past. Evan had told Chris almost every shameful, dirty thing.

"I have nothing to hide."

"Fine. If you don't want to talk about it, I won't force the issue." She turned from him, donning her sunglasses, then studied the activity out on the pavement. They'd chosen to sit outside to enjoy the warm day. Midafternoon Honolulu boasted businessmen and women rushing to their next meeting, their Bluetooth earpieces in place. Mothers were walking their babies among the ever-present tourists roaming the area. Evan sensed that she wasn't really interested in it.

"Cynthia."

She faced him. He wished he could read her eyes, but they

were hidden behind the dark lenses. She said nothing. The tension grew between them but she didn't move to fill the silence. Instead, she seemed to be challenging him to some kind of stare down. And, although he was well known for his poker face, he didn't have the time or patience to mess around.

"What?"

She hesitated before answering. "I thought we were here for Chris."

He dipped his head. "Agreed."

"Then why are you acting like some superficial jackass?"

The bite in her voice surprised him. He'd been pushing her buttons, and being, well, a jackass. He'd wanted to get a rise out of her and he got it. But the absolute authority lacing her question momentarily stunned him. Evan might have been wrong thinking she couldn't take to her role. This wasn't the mouse of a woman he'd met in Chris's restaurant. Her posture spoke of a woman in control, with new confidence. Chris's request for this lunch now made more sense.

When he didn't answer, she continued. "You want to act like that? Fine. Just let me know. But for some reason Chris wants us to know each other better. Why, I have no idea. Probably because we both mean a lot to him."

Evan understood why, but he was sure that Cynthia didn't. Knowing Chris, he hadn't revealed his ultimate fantasy. It pleased Evan to see her so secure with her burgeoning Domme. Still, being a Dom himself, the behavior nicked at his temper.

"And so you think that for some reason I should open my heart to you over sweet tea and lunch?"

She stood and grabbed her purse. With a shove to her chair, she whipped around to leave. Irritation and regret warred within him. High maintenance women—with their demands for attention and soul-searching conversation—were not his cup of

169

tea. He preferred the straightforward approach. When a woman like Cynthia flounced off, it was better to enjoy the view as they left. But she was what Chris wanted, what he thought he needed. Owing his life to the man was getting damned inconvenient.

"Cynthia!"

She paused, but didn't give him the courtesy of turning around.

"I apologize. Please stay." He bit each painful word out.

She didn't react to his plea. Not right away. Annoyance crawled under his skin, an uncomfortable irritation. Women didn't think about refusing a request or demand from him. They begged for his attention, good or bad.

"I promise to behave."

Cynthia glanced back over her shoulder at him, her eyes narrowing as she studied his face. "I doubt very much you behave often, if ever."

He gave her a look of mock innocence. Her laughter allowed some of the muscles in his stomach to relax. She eased back into her chair, setting her purse on the one beside her.

"I didn't mean to upset you. Truly." He tried to appear sincere, because he was, but he couldn't sound completely contrite.

"I know. And I'd say I didn't mean to pry but we both know I'd be lying. But as someone who pretended to be someone she wasn't for most of her life, I know it when I see it."

He leaned back as their plates were set in front of them. "Why does it matter to you that I do? That is, if I do."

"Mainly because your public personality reminds me too much of my brother."

Oh, that wasn't good. Sisterly feelings might put a crimp

into Chris's plans. "And that's bad because..."

She bit into her sandwich and hummed her pleasure. Lust coiled in his belly. Images of having her mouth on his dick, the vibrations of that action skimming across his flesh, his balls drawing up tight...

Shifting in his seat to ease the ache, he waited as she daintily wiped some sauce from her mouth.

"My brother is a bastard." Blunt and to the point. The blush stealing up her neck ruined the boldness of her words.

"I take it you two aren't close."

She shook her head. "I could say that it's because we're several years apart in age. But it's more that he's just a bastard. He was raised to be one."

He nodded. "So, you think I'm really a good guy underneath the bastard personality."

She choked on a sip of water. "I didn't say you had a bastard personality. I said that's the way you act." Cynthia set her glass down. "My brother's personality is just that. Self-serving. You're not like that."

"So, you think that everything I do is for a higher purpose?"

"No. I would never say that. But I do think you use it to keep people at a distance. I also have a feeling that you don't do that with Chris, or he wouldn't be your friend."

The woman was too perceptive for her own good, but he had to concede she was right, especially about his best friend. Still, he didn't like her getting too close and he definitely resented her assumptions. "And so you want to get to know the real me?"

"I'm not sure if I want to get to know you at all. But the truth is, Chris wants it, or needs it for some reason, and he never asks anything of me. I want to do this for him if it will ease whatever worry he has."

The truth and sincerity in her voice touched something in him. Cynthia recognized a need in Chris that had taken Evan years to realize. Chris worked overtime for sick employees, arranged work around people's school schedules, and handled his family's squabbles. Whatever you needed, he strove to offer it to you. He never questioned your reasons, your lifestyle...he just accepted. In return, Chris asked for nothing. He'd saved Evan, literally picked him up out of the gutter more than once, and in return Chris wanted nothing but his friendship. A nurturer at heart, Chris had been searching high and low for someone to shower with that love and attention. Evan had worried that Chris would get tangled up with a woman who'd bleed him dry and leave him. For the first time in weeks, Evan was getting the feeling that Chris had chosen wisely.

He smiled, this time with genuine happiness. Cynthia blinked, then returned the gesture, although her smile was a bit wary.

"You're right. About me, about Chris." He took a bite of his sandwich and chewed it, never taking his gaze from hers. "But there are reasons."

"I understand. But take it from someone who was a world champion in pretending to be someone you're not. One of these days, it will bite you in the butt."

He chuckled. "That isn't always a bad thing, Ms. Cynthia."

She snorted. "You would know."

Easy with her now, he relaxed against the back of his chair and stretched his legs out. "So, I hear you went to that sucky school in Athens," he said, referring to the University of Georgia.

She wrinkled her nose. "Better than being a loser from USC."

Every true Southerner understood college rivalry. "We had a saying in Columbia about Georgia. Something about how they picked the mascot because it reminded them of their girlfriends."

She shrugged off the insult of being compared to a bulldog. "Yeah, well I still say it's better than a school with a penis for a mascot."

His laughter turned the heads of several patrons but he didn't care. It had been a long time since he'd traded insults with another Southerner. Enjoying himself, he dug into his coleslaw and launched into reasons why South Carolina was superior to Georgia.

The front door to Dupree's opened, and Cynthia's laughter drifted over the music. Chris turned toward the sound, releasing a sigh of relief. Evan's arm draped over her shoulders as she giggled at something he said.

"I'm telling you. Georgia just got lucky that year. They should've never made it into the playoffs."

She rolled her eyes. "Give it up. USC couldn't beat their way out of a paper bag."

Evan threw back his head and laughed, more relaxed than Chris had seen him in months. The tension that had been niggling the back of his mind since Cynthia had left eased.

"Looks like you two had a good time."

She smiled at him. "Went to one of your competitors. I have to say, they do have a way with Carolina Barbeque."

Placing her hands on the bar, she lifted herself up and leaned over to give him a kiss. She jumped up on one of the barstools, settling her elbows on the counter. "How're things going here?"

The warmth of her breath still tingled over his lips, scrambling his thoughts. It took him a second or two to answer. "Okay. Had a bit of a problem with a customer who must've started drinking at eight in the morning. But May handled it."

"May can fix anything," Evan remarked, smiling at the woman in question. She offered him a vague look then walked away.

"What the hell was that about?" Evan asked, still watching May as she sauntered to the back of the restaurant.

Chris shrugged. Sharp as a tack, Evan could work the most complex figures out in his head. If he couldn't understand why May was mad at him, Chris didn't want to be the one who told him.

Cynthia slid off the stool. "I gotta get going. Mike wanted to show me another property for rent in Hawaii Kai."

He frowned at her. "That's some pricey real estate."

She smirked at him. "Spoken by a man who owns a home in the area." Giving him another quick, hard kiss that had his head fogging and his body humming, she smiled at him. "It must be within my price range or Mike wouldn't have suggested it. I have some shopping to do after I get done. Wanna meet back here for dinner? I won't even mooch off ya. My treat."

That was a bit too smooth of an offer, but he let it go. "Sure. Whatever you want."

"Good, because I'm stealing May."

May walked out of the back, her purse in her hands. She tossed Chris a lethal smile. "Don't worry about Chris. He knows better than to say anything. I'll leave him high and dry."

Cynthia turned to Evan. "Thank you for lunch." She rose to

her tiptoes and brushed her lips over his cheek. "Even if it was ruined by the stench of a USC fan."

She waved her fingers then slipped her hand through May's arm and walked out of the restaurant.

"You know, if you hadn't snapped her up, I might've taken her for a ride."

Chris glanced over at his friend. "Really? Good girls aren't your cup of tea."

His attention still fixed on where the two women had last been in view, Evan said, "Yeah, but there's something about her. Something about how proper she acts and how she is with you. It'd be mighty fun to strip away all that good-girl veneer to see the naughty woman beneath."

"Hey!"

Evan shook himself and glanced over his shoulder with a grin. "Even if I wanted her, that woman is stuck on you. Damn, it was disgusting the way she gets all goo-goo eyed when she talks about you."

Chris smiled, warmth curling into his heart. "Yeah?"

"Ick. Yeah, just like that. You two are disgusting."

"Come on, have a drink, on me."

He nodded. "Give me a Dr. Pepper."

"So everything went okay?" He filled a glass and set it on the bar in front of Evan.

Evan took a healthy gulp. "No problems. Sure doesn't take any crap."

"What did you do?"

Evan's eyes widened. "How did you know I did something?"

Chris arched one eyebrow.

"Okay, I tried to talk smack. Didn't fly."

Chris scratched his chin. "Yeah, I can imagine that it didn't."

"You didn't tell me she was so smart, not to mention that nasty temper."

Chris paused in wiping the counter. Cynthia did have a temper she rarely showed and only to those people she trusted. She held back her true personality traits because of her lack of confidence in her abilities.

"Well, that's impressive."

"That I pissed off your woman? Not really. Seems to be something I'm good at."

Chris started his chore again. "No. It's good. She wouldn't have stood up to you if she hadn't felt comfortable with you."

"Then mission accomplished. Last week she looked like she was waiting for me to pounce on her, but if that kiss is anything to judge by, she doesn't have any more worries."

"Yeah, I noticed that kiss."

Evan looked down at his glass. "It was nothing."

For a moment, Chris couldn't say anything. His mind was frozen on the fact that Evan Chambers, who'd had enough sexual escapades to make a seasoned whore blush, was sitting at his bar embarrassed by a little kiss.

"Is there something wrong?"

"No." He studied his glass for a second longer before taking another sip. "Have you told her about us?"

"Us? I had no idea you had feelings for me."

Evan's lips quirked before he looked at Chris. "Smartass. I mean about us sharing women."

Chris rubbed the back of his neck. "No, not yet. It isn't like we did it that often and that was before I stopped going to Rough 'n' Ready."

Evan's smile turned evil. "It wouldn't be because you're avoiding telling her, is it?"

"Maybe. Part of me wants to tell her, but then another part of me is afraid I'll freak her out."

"I think Ms. Cynthia is more than able to handle something like that. The longer you put it off, the worse it will get."

Uncomfortable with the subject, Chris decided to change it. "Yeah, seems like you two learned a lot about each other. I mean, before she left, she didn't even want to have lunch with you. Now, you're like kissing cousins."

"Shut up." Evan frowned, took another long gulp of his drink and slammed it down on the bar. "I gotta go."

He abruptly stood and strode out of the restaurant, completely ignoring a rather well-built blonde. Not only did he not notice the woman, but he let the front door slam in her face.

Chris chuckled. It was about time Evan had his world tilted sideways. His friend saw women in black and white, good or bad. There was no in between for him.

He shook away his thoughts of Evan as he walked back to the office. He'd been worried over the lunch. Worried that Cynthia would refuse, or that Evan would offend her in some way, completely on purpose. If their relationship remained awkward, his plans would be ruined. She didn't hate Evan, but she'd never seemed to relax around him until today.

As he let himself into his office, Chris turned over the next problem to solve. He had to be patient enough to allow Cynthia to complete her journey. Submitting was something within him he wanted to give her, but the part of him that wanted—needed—to dominate her itched to be set free. It clawed his belly and roared through his blood.

With a sigh, he dropped into his chair. He would force himself to accommodate her development. The changes in her the last several weeks were too precious to jeopardize with his eagerness to complete their journey.

He prayed it was damn soon, or he might just go insane.

Chapter Fourteen

As Michelle placed their meals in front of them later that night, Chris resisted the urge to growl. *Aroused* didn't even begin to describe how he felt. When he'd seen the way Cynthia was dressed, the way the black fabric clung to her curves, the sexy thigh-high boots, the only thought he'd had was to strip her naked—leaving the boots on of course—and fuck her. What was pushing him closer to the edge was her little game. That Cynthia had decided to play the role of a complete Domme was as exciting as it was irritating.

She leaned forward, closed her eyes and drew in a deep breath, affording Chris an excellent view of her cleavage.

"Hmm, something sure smells good." After making that statement, she sat back, the satisfied smile on her face telling him she knew just what she was doing. She twirled the linguine around her fork and raised it to her mouth, then stopped, looking at his plate. "Aren't you going to eat?"

Chris comforted himself with the thought that this would somehow pay off in the end. Without a word, he picked up his fork and dug into his meal.

"You know, I didn't think you would take this so badly, Chris."

He swallowed his fish before answering. "Take what so badly? Being teased?"

She pushed her lower lip out in a perfect pout. "I'm not teasing you."

"What do you call it?"

She blinked, apparently taken aback by his irritated tone. "Foreplay."

He would give her that. But if she kept pushing him, he wouldn't make it through dinner. He was amazed the table wasn't rising from the erection she'd inspired. They ate in silence for a few minutes, then she sat back in her chair and studied him.

"I'm confused. You said you wanted this, that this would be good for me."

He had. He just hadn't known she would take to the role so well. It was a dream come true, but as his mamma said, he should be careful what he wished for.

"I'm frustrated." He could barely bite out the words.

She smiled, and just like the first time he'd seen her smile all those months ago in Georgia, he was mesmerized. When she truly smiled, her dimples came out in full force, and it never failed to make his heart flip over. As sappy as it sounded, it made him feel like he owned the world.

"You've been a bit of a baby about it, but then I have to say you did have a few good moments. I think that deserves some kind of reward." She sipped her wine. "Why don't you tell me what you'd like to do tonight?"

"I told you."

She sighed, pulling on the bottom of her sweater. Her hardened nipples pressed against the knit fabric.

"I'd like to find out if you're wearing anything beneath that outfit."

"What do you think?"

He studied her intently, looking for any hint of a bra. "I don't think you're wearing anything."

She smiled, coyly this time. "Why, Mr. Dupree, are you saying I would run around without anything on beneath my clothes?"

Another wave of lust spiraled through his blood as it rushed to his groin. Her voice had deepened into that upper-crust Georgia accent he loved so much. She used it to tease him.

"Ms. Myers, I do believe you would."

Her smile widened, her eyes sparkling. "Thank you."

"For what?"

"I doubt anyone I know would think that I'd run around braless."

"They don't know you as well as I do."

She crossed her arms beneath her breasts and leaned forward. Her gaze never wavered as she said, "Why don't you give that pretty, fat cock a stroke for me?"

He dropped his fork on his plate, his body going rigid. She'd been gaining her ground in domination, but this was public. Chris hadn't anticipated her taking this step—definitely not so soon.

She sat back, a frown puckering the skin between her sculpted eyebrows. "Are you not going to do what I say?"

Immediately, he slipped his hand beneath the table, thankful they had tablecloths at Dupree's, and gave his shaft a long, leisurely stroke. As his fingers moved over the fabric of his jeans, he closed his eyes, enjoying the sweet torture. It didn't even get close to helping, as the stiff fabric made it difficult to apply the right pressure. Still, it was better than nothing.

"That's enough."

It wasn't, but he obeyed and put his hands back on the table.

"Very good. You know, we talk about all my fantasies, what I would like, but we rarely talk about yours. What is your ultimate fantasy?"

His brain stopped working. Mainly because every ounce of blood had drained down to his shaft, but now she wanted him to talk about fantasies. His first instinct was to grab her and run to the nearest dark corner and fuck her. But he fought it because he knew this was significant. "I'd like to share you."

She cocked her head to one side and studied him again. "Share me? I don't understand."

At first, he was convinced she was screwing with him again. But he looked beyond his own out-of-control lust and saw the confusion. At least it hadn't been fear. "I would like to share you with another man."

She took a sip of her wine and said nothing. At least she hadn't run screaming from the restaurant. After she swallowed her wine, she said, "I've never even thought about something like that." She smiled. "Are you ready to go?"

He nodded, and she motioned to Michelle, handing over her credit card. As they waited for Michelle to return, she teased him with details of their night, leaving out enough information to keep him wondering.

"I think tonight we should go to my place." She smiled after that statement. It was only twenty minutes to his house, a possible forty to hers. "I've been...shopping. I think you'll like what I bought you."

Intrigued, he wanted to ask what it was, but he refrained. Delight sparkled in her eyes that he'd behaved.

After she signed the receipt, she rose slowly. He waited, not rising until she indicated he had permission.

"Come, Chris."

He followed her out, walking several paces behind her, trying to keep his gaze everywhere but her swaying ass. It was just not possible. Before she'd started learning about roles in the D/s world, she'd reduced him to a puddle of lust. But now, he was a slavering he-man, ready to do her bidding. Within minutes they were speeding along H-1 in her car, Chris driving.

She kept the conversation light but continually touched him. A stroke on his thigh, her fingers sliding down his bare arm. By the time they reached her house, he didn't think he'd be able to walk, he was in so much pain. After he parked the car, she waited for him to open her door.

Cynthia ascended the steps with Chris tailing after her. With the distance between them, and the difference in their heights, he was eye level with her rear end. The sun had set and the only light came from her porch light and the street lights. Even with that little bit of illumination, he could tell she wasn't wearing any panties. Lord, have mercy.

Unlocking the door, she led him into her living area. As usual, he removed his shoes and left them by the door, but he noticed she didn't remove her boots. Anticipation crawled through him. He'd hoped she'd leave them on.

She dropped her purse onto the coffee table, then grabbed his hand, slowly leading him back to her bedroom. Once there, she sat on her bed and smiled. Again his heart did that strange little flip when he saw the self-assured light in her eyes. This was a true Domme in her element.

She leaned back on her elbows, crossed her legs and said, "Come here."

Cynthia licked her lips as Chris approached. Her palms itched to touch the ripple of muscle beneath his shirt.

Excitement and nerves threatened her ability to think straight. She was so sure it would come out as a request and not a demand when she'd said it. Instead, her voice rang with authority. She'd taken control before, but this was a different aspect. He'd wear the bindings she'd bought for him. She wanted him to understand that tonight was significant.

He walked with slow, steady steps. She smiled to herself. He was testing her, seeing how far she would go. He just didn't know how far she wanted to go.

When he finally stood in front of her, she waited a moment before moving. Her body hummed, needing a release. But she denied herself that. He'd take her orders happily, but the significance of the evening was too great to rush it. She wanted to stretch out the anticipation for both of them.

Her body rubbed against his as she stood. He didn't say a word, but his breathing hitched as she allowed her hand to move over his hardened cock. Even through the thick jean material, he was impressive.

Stepping to his side, she said, "Lose your shirt."

He paused, grabbed hold of the shirt and tugged it off. She sighed over the beauty of his body. She shouldn't be so shallow, but she couldn't stop the thrill she felt in looking him over. Muscles flexed as he lowered his arms then tossed the shirt behind him. *Ahh, he's definitely making this fun.* Chris so loved testing her resolve. Before tonight, he usually won. This evening was different, would change everything in her mind. A surge of heat coiled in her stomach.

"Please pick that up and fold it."

He obeyed immediately.

"And remember to do that from now on. You know better. Now, the pants."

Unhurriedly, he unbuttoned and unzipped his jeans. He

pulled them down and folded them, placing them on the dresser on top of his shirt. His erection pressed against his knit boxer shorts, a telltale circle of wetness near the head of his penis.

"You've been very good." She smiled at him. "You may remove my boots."

She motioned for him to sit on the bed. When he complied, she lifted her foot, placing it on the mattress between his legs. He tugged on the zipper. As he slid it down, he slipped his fingers between the leather and her skin. A rush of tingles followed the motion, her head spinning with a heady mix of arousal and adrenaline. She didn't call him on the extra touching, just looked down at him and frowned. Stepping back, she put the other foot up. He did the exact same thing. If it hadn't felt so good, she would have punished him, but he had been so sneaky in the way that he'd done it, she decided to let it slip by this time.

"Stand up."

He obeyed, but didn't jump to his feet. Bit by bit, he unfolded his length. As he rose, their bodies brushed, just as she had done to him earlier. She could've stepped back, but it would have been a sign of weakness. The fabric of her dress moved over her breasts. Her hardened nipples drew tighter. By the time he was standing upright, his erection pressed against her stomach, and both of them were breathing deeper.

He was pushing her, testing her, and dammit, she was creaming. Her pussy lips dripped with her juices. Part of this was their game. She'd learned over the last few weeks that Chris might like to submit, but he didn't go quietly.

Neither of them said a word as he kept his gaze averted. If anyone had seen him, they might say he was the picture of the perfect sub. But she knew better. He fairly vibrated with the need to grab her and throw her on the bed behind him. But he wouldn't, unless she asked.

"Chris."

He raised his gaze to hers. Desire, lust, whatever you wanted to call it, darkened his eyes, bringing out the golden sparks within their depths. She wanted his submission and the look of quiet defiance in his expression told her she would have to demand it. Worry prickled down her spine but she fought it away. Chris had to sense she was ready for this or he wouldn't push.

She took a decisive step back, letting him know she wasn't fooled by the innocent look he was giving her. "Now your boxers."

Her voice had grown throatier and he smiled. Still, he did her bidding. Once he had them off, he stood before her, completely nude and completely beautiful.

Would she ever get used to seeing him naked? Would she ever get used to the fact that he was hers for the taking? Probably not. Of course he was ready for her, as always. His cock, already hard and thick, curved up to his stomach. She couldn't resist reaching out and brushing her thumb over the tip. After swiping the pearl of cum off, she lifted her thumb to her mouth and licked. He groaned, but she ignored him, enjoying the salty taste of him.

"Hmm, you taste good, but I tell you that all the time."

He didn't say anything, but his nostrils flared, and his fingers curled into his palms. This was killing him, the poor baby.

"You've been pretty good, so I will reward you."

She stepped back, needing the space, and pulled her shirt up over her head. By the time she could see him again, his eyes were feasting on the sight of her bare breasts. The cool air washed over her sensitized skin, combining with his heated

186

gaze, and her control slipped a bit. Trying her best to ignore the need to touch, to jump him and use his body for her pleasure, she drew in a deep breath.

"Lie down on the bed, big boy. I have a present for you."

He hesitated. His gaze dipped to her breasts, and he licked his lips.

She chuckled. "If you're a good boy."

He climbed onto the bed. She opened her dresser drawer and pulled out the set of cuffs she'd bought earlier that day. When Chris saw what she held in her hands, his eyes darkened and his breathing hitched. The fact that he realized the significance of them warmed her heart. He was the one man who understood her. He comprehended her needs and wants even before she knew what she needed. How could she not love him for taking her for who she was and allowing her to become the woman she wanted to be?

She blinked back tears, knowing this wasn't the time to get sentimental. Placing the restraints on the table, she shimmied out of her skirt, happy to see the way he watched her every motion, his attention moving to her pussy. She'd kept herself shaved bare, because she knew he liked it. It left her flesh sensitive to every movement, more aware of her excitement. Her choice to go without panties had been twofold. She liked the feeling of not wearing anything under her clothes—there was something very freeing about it. The second reason was the skirt she'd worn. The way the fabric had clung to her, Chris had to wonder about the absence of panty lines.

Without a word to him, she grabbed the cuffs, climbed onto the bed and straddled him. She leaned forward and her breasts grazed his chest. His breath warmed her skin as she unsnapped the cuff and slipped it over his wrist. She threaded the chain that linked the two pieces of leather between the slats of her headboard. With that done, she latched his free wrist with the remaining cuff. When she finished, she slipped her fingers beneath each restraint to make sure they weren't too tight. Then she sat up, bearing down on his hardened shaft. She flexed her hips, allowing her cream to wet his dick. He groaned, causing her to smile. She couldn't wait to get that thick cock inside of her, but she wanted to play a bit more.

She touched her mouth to his, sliding her tongue in to mate with his. Hips gyrating, she moved against his cock and had to control the impulse to press harder, to push herself over the edge. She was close. Another gush of cream wet her pussy. Pulling away from the kiss, Cynthia shifted down his body, licking and nipping her way along, enjoying the salty taste of his skin and the scent of his cologne. She reached his penis and sighed. Before meeting Chris, she'd had little to no interest in cocks, or the way they looked. But from their first night, she had become obsessed.

The darkened flared head of it was wet with another drop of liquid. The pearly color of it contrasted against his mocha-colored skin. She wrapped her hand around the base of his cock and began stroking.

"Ahh, that's nice, Chris. You do have the most gorgeous cock." The cum dripped down one side of his cock and she licked it off. Reaching beneath him, she glided her hand over his scrotum and was rewarded when his shaft jerked in her hand.

"Now, let's see if I can make you happy."

Chris had thought Cynthia would be dangerous when she realized her potential. He'd miscalculated just *how* dangerous. Damn, she was driving him crazy. She'd slowed her rhythm, which had pushed him close to fulfillment, but kept him hovering, not allowing him to go over.

She licked his cockhead again, her tongue pausing over the hole. He closed his eyes and shuddered.

"Open your eyes." He did as she ordered, looking down the length of his body. "I want you to watch, and remember, don't come unless I tell you."

Holy Christ, this was hell. He couldn't move his hands to touch her. He'd never been so turned on in his life, or so frustrated. What she was doing to him was only half of it. Seeing her take control, the sound of her voice as she stated what she wanted, the way she held herself—they all added up to one major turn on. That, coupled with the magic she was performing with her mouth and hands... He was amazed he didn't pass out on the spot.

He'd known he loved her, but he'd had no idea just how it would feel to have her claim him in this way. He'd been ready since the moment she stepped into his kitchen...no, since the moment he first saw her in Georgia. He'd known she was the one for him. Deep in his soul, he'd recognized her. Now, she knew, she understood that he was hers. Tenderness and desire blended, threading its way through his veins. Temptation to let go, to just give in to the primal need clawing at his belly, almost overwhelmed him.

Lowering her head, she took the very tip of his dick in her mouth, swiped her tongue over it again and hummed. *Holy fucking hell!* The vibrations pulsed down his cock, past his balls and spread throughout his body. Her tongue swiped over the head again, then she slipped him further into her mouth. As her plump, pink lips took him in, he groaned. He thrashed his legs as she deep throated him. With each brush against the back of her throat, his body raced closer.

She released him and sat up. The smile curving her lips

touched his heart as much as it frustrated him.

"You need to stay still, Chris. You're distracting me."

A growl simmered in the pit of his soul. He wanted to touch, to taste. The need to take her, drive into her heated core burned within him. He twisted his wrists slightly, curling his fingers into his palms. Her gaze immediately focused on the movement.

"Those aren't too tight, are they?" Her tone had softened, her worry warming his heart.

"No. Cynthia—"

"Then don't move." All sweetness and light gone. That did more to spike his arousal than the soft concern of her question.

Her eyes narrowed as she settled on his groin. "You're not behaving."

The ability to talk had dissolved the moment her heated cunt rested against his shaft. She was dripping, wetting his dick. She smiled as he said nothing. "That's better. Now, I think I need a little something in return for all my hard work."

She scooted up his body, stopping when her sex hovered over his mouth. Her pussy lips glistened, showing her excitement, the scent of her filling his senses. Wrapping her hands around the headboard, she lowered herself to his mouth.

With a groan, he dove between her lips, enjoying the sweetness of her essence. It was difficult to maneuver with his hands still restrained, but he drove his tongue up and in her over and over. He flicked it over her hardened clit, and she trembled. Her thighs shook next to his face. Pleasure thrummed through him as he continued feasting. Her muscles tightened, her moans grew, but before he could tumble her over the edge, she lifted her body away.

The bed dipped as she leaned over and grabbed something

off the table. She straddled him again, her hands shaking enough to give him satisfaction. She ripped open a condom wrapper. Pinching the end of it, she rolled it down his shaft then mounted him. He closed his eyes, enjoying the feel of her muscles grasping his cock. Damn, she was slick, wetter than he'd ever felt her.

"Watch."

He opened his eyes. When their gazes met, she began to move. "Oh, yes, oh, Chris."

Her muscles contracted, signaling the approach of her orgasm and pulling him deeper. "Fuck me, Chris, do it."

With that order, and the feel of her pussy squeezing his dick, he exploded, jerking his pelvis upward as she slammed down on him. She continued to move, milking his orgasm and triggering her own.

"Chris, baby, yes." She threw her head back, her body arching. A primal, unintelligible moan ripped from her throat as she shuddered. The sight of Cynthia in her fulfillment held Chris mesmerized until she collapsed on top of him.

A moment later she fumbled with the cuffs, releasing him. He still pulsed within her as her body completely relaxed into sleep. Skimming his hand down her spine, he cupped her ass. Not too shabby for a first-time Domme. True, she hadn't taken it as far as she could have, but Lord knew, any further might have killed him.

Now that she had discovered her dominant side, would she be willing to give it up to explore submission?

A week later, Cynthia and Chris sat on his lanai, enjoying a mild afternoon, watching the waves and the windsurfers below. She'd never felt so complete, she thought, as she leaned against him and sipped at her margarita. If a year ago someone had told her she would enjoy anal sex and handcuffing her partner to the bed, Cynthia would have written them off as insane.

On top of that, they seemed to have grown closer, both of them accepting her nature for what it was. Each time they made love, the connection between them grew stronger. She knew from what Chris had taught her, and what she gained from reading, that trust was a key element of submission. Chris's complete acceptance of her, of what she needed, forged a connection she'd never had with another man.

"Remember the first night you arrived, when I told you about being a switch?" Chris asked.

She nodded and took another drink, allowing her muscles to relax further. The search for a new bakery location had been aggravating. If one storefront was too expensive, another had a horrible location. She was determined to find the right place, but the wait was irritating her. Chris had been understanding, accompanying her as much as possible to offer his opinions.

"I said I liked to play the role of both the submissive and the dominant, remember?"

Something in his tone sent alarm shooting down Cynthia's spine. Sitting up, she turned and faced him. The expression on his face had her worried.

"Yes, I remember." She barely got the words out. Fear was clogging her throat as she tried to figure out just what he was getting at. They'd made love almost every night for the last two months, and not once had he complained. In fact, he seemed not to be able to get enough of her.

"Well, I want to try that with you."

Wary now, she pulled further away and studied him. He

took her margarita glass out of her hands and placed it on the ground beside her, then pressed her hands between his.

"What I saw in you, what I understood about you from the beginning, is that you might be a switch like me."

She shook her head, but he nodded.

"Generally, before you become a Domme you would have experienced being a sub. But I did it differently with you. You weren't...ready for that."

"I don't understand."

Panic was now running full force through her blood. She'd known he would ask this. In all her reading, she had come to understand not only her own wants and desires, but those Chris had. She knew that for them to stay together, he would need this part of her. But she hadn't expected it so soon.

He met her gaze and said, "I love you, Cynthia. I think I have since I saw you burst into that dressing room at the church. But what I want—no, what I *need*—is for you to relinquish your dominant role."

Fear slapped at her defenses. She didn't want to lose this part of her character. "I-I'm not sure."

"You know now what it means, what I need. What you need too."

"I'm not sure you're right, Chris." She pulled in a shaky breath. "I understand, but I'm not sure I can give it to you."

She untangled her hand from his. She didn't want him to know how much he had shaken her.

"No. I need..." She swallowed and closed her eyes. When she opened them, she gazed directly into his. "I need time. I know that I should have expected it, and I did. I just didn't expect it so soon. I don't know if I'm ready."

"It is about trust, Cynthia. If you trust me, you will give me this." Just as he did for her. He left the words unspoken but the truth lay between them. He had trusted her enough, a Domme who was learning her way, and had accepted her. Now all he asked was if she could return that favor.

"I—"

"I need this from you. For us to be complete, we need this. I want Evan—"

"You want me to give up the power I've gained. Don't you understand what that will mean for me?" The hitch in her voice when she asked the question embarrassed her. He had to know this wasn't easy, that this could destroy her.

Without blinking, he said, "Yes."

His confidence, his arrogance shook her. She rose from her position and gathered her purse.

"Where are you going?"

She turned back to him, trying to cling to her composure. Cynthia didn't want him to see her anxiety. It was silly, but she wanted to hold onto her pride for a little while longer.

"I hope you understand I need time to think." He opened his mouth to argue, but she placed her fingers over his lips. "Please. You know I understand. I've read more books about the subject than you probably have. I just..." She shook her head. "Give me a little time."

She could tell from the look in his eyes he wasn't happy with the request, but he nodded. Rising to her tiptoes, she replaced her fingers with her mouth, trying her best to let him know that she loved him. She poured her heart, her soul, into the kiss. Slipping her tongue into his mouth, she savored the tangy sweet taste of the margaritas they'd been drinking. Before she wanted to, she drew back.

"I'll call you."

Again, he said nothing but nodded. She fought the urge to run back and jump into his arms, to do what he wanted, but she required this time to think.

Without another word, she walked away. Each step caused a crack in her heart, her soul. She didn't break until she was driving down H-1. Tears scalded the backs of her eyes as she blinked to keep them from spilling over. In her life she had never felt so exposed, so vulnerable.

Concentrating on her driving, she tried her best to put her thoughts aside until she got home. There would be plenty of time to contemplate her future with Chris. She needed space to gain perspective. Still she couldn't quite stop the tears that continued to well up. He'd struck at the foundation she had been building since she defied her father, and she didn't know if she would ever be able to gather the pieces back together again.

Thirty minutes later she pulled into her carport and noticed someone on her porch. When she stepped out of her car, a man stood and her heart dropped to her stomach. Her father. She looked toward the street and saw the rental car parked beside her mailbox.

Well, today just keeps getting better. She walked up the steps to the porch, but didn't say a word. They just stared at each other, in a silent contest to see who would crack first. She was pleasantly surprised with the result.

"I was wondering when you'd get home."

Her father's tone held a note of censure, but she ignored it. "What are you doing here, Father?"

"I'm here to take you home."

"I'm home now."

"Don't be ridiculous. This isn't your home. Your mother has been beside herself." The practiced sincerity in his voice sickened her. Not so much that he resorted to it so readily, but

195

the fact she'd accepted it all her life. So needy for affection, she accepted false emotion instead of demanding the real thing.

Cynthia shook her head, sadness bearing down on her. She rode the thin edge of control. Her emotions had been out of whack since her conversation with Chris and before she'd had a chance to think about his request, her father appeared, demanding her attention. Life sucked.

"I was in Georgia for my thirtieth birthday. No one contacted me." She sent him a disgusted look. "You don't care about me, you care about the money I inherited."

"It has nothing to do with the money."

"Really?" She crossed her arms beneath her breasts. She could tell her father was a little taken aback by her behavior. Usually by now she was doing whatever he wanted. No scenes. No emotional outbursts.

"Who told you that it was about the money? Max?" His cold eyes narrowed as he studied her. "Or was it that slime you're fucking?"

Again, anger built within her. She might have left everything up in the air about their relationship, but her father would not put down the man she loved. The man she needed.

"I'd use my words carefully, if I were you." A normal person would hear the threat in her tone, but her father was warming up to his subject and didn't take note.

"I know what you've been doing, shopping in stores filled with trash, and now you're sleeping with trash. You should be ashamed of yourself. You're no different than your grandmother."

Her throat burned with the need to yell at him, but she refused to let him see how much he'd hurt her. How much she still wanted his acceptance, knowing she would never receive that, let alone love.

She took a step closer and was pleased to see him take a step back in reaction. "Listen, Father. The days when you could tell me what to do, who to do and when to do it are over. The day you threw me out of the house because I wanted to attend a wedding sealed your fate. And for your information, what I find disgusting is your need to spy on your daughter."

She swept past him, but he grabbed her arm, hard. His fingers dug into the tender flesh of her upper arm.

"You will do what I say. I need that money."

As she studied the anger on his face, an ache welled in her heart. For years she'd tried to please him. Nothing had ever been good enough, never would be. He would never accept her for who she was, and she was tired of trying. Jerking her arm away, hoping that the police officer who lived across the street was watching the whole thing, she leaned closer to his face.

"You have no right to my money. You made your bed, you lie in it. If you show up here again, I'll call the police."

She turned and unlocked her door, knowing he was watching her every move, probably too confused to think. Without saying anything else, she stepped into her house, shut the door and locked it. Leaning against it, she held her breath. Moments later, she heard him walk down the steps and his car start up. Her cell phone rang. It was Charlie, the cop across the street. After reassuring him that everything was all right, she hung up, then collapsed on her papasan chair.

Closing her eyes, she tried to block out the day's events, but couldn't. Her father's visit—not to see if she was okay, but to get her money. She sighed as a few tears welled up in her eyes. It was wrong, but it still hurt to know her father saw her only as a means to an end.

Her mind turned to Chris. The expression he wore when he asked her to trust him, to give him what he had given her still twisted her in the gut. Unwillingly, the stark pain on his face, the devastation, now registered. He hadn't called, hadn't followed her. Knowing she needed space, he'd let her go. She understood without being told that he had left everything up to her.

She opened her eyes and jerked upward. He'd left it up to her.

He didn't demand. In the end, even after he'd asked for her submission, he had not told her what he wanted. He'd *asked*.

Drawing in a deep breath, she began to turn over the memories of the last few months. They'd shared secrets, desires. The night in his restaurant when she'd asked him of his ultimate fantasy danced through her mind. He'd told her that night, in simple terms. She'd dismissed it, thinking nothing of it after the conversation. What if that was what he wanted now?

He'd mentioned something about Evan, but it hadn't registered. She'd been so freaked out by his request of relinquishing her dominance that she'd ignored his other comments. What if he'd been trying to tell her he wanted to share her with Evan? It would explain why he'd wanted them to be friendlier. She sorted through the idea, thinking of the implications of agreeing to it.

Instead of anger or disgust, lust pumped through her at the thought. Two men? She tugged her bottom lip between her teeth, waiting for the denial to come—for the disgust to set in—but it didn't.

She *was* aroused by the idea. In fact, she was really, really aroused by it. She shivered as her nipples hardened. Fear had pushed her to panic, but now...now she understood. Love, trust, submission...all of it she wanted to offer to him. She loved him without reservation. That gave her the courage, the need to accept his request.

Chapter Fifteen

Chris pulled some green peppers out of the bin, shut the drawer and let the fridge door shut. He was still in the process of chastising himself for the way he'd handled Cynthia. As he washed the peppers, he thought about their argument. Stupid. Impatient and stupid.

Drawing out a knife, he began to chop the peppers. He had lost his patience with her and blurted out his intent. He'd known she understood what he needed. Still, he should have eased her into it, given her time to accept that to complete their connection, her submission, her trust was needed.

Watching her develop her control over him had been more of a turn-on than he'd expected, but then he'd blown it. Instead of gently introducing her to the idea, he'd demanded it, like an ass. Lord only knew what she would say when she found out he'd planned on having Evan join them.

As he turned on the heat under his sauté pan, the doorbell rang. He knew it wasn't Cynthia. She had her own key. When he opened the door, he found Evan standing on the porch.

"I went by the restaurant, and they said you called in." His gaze searched Chris's. "You sick?"

"No, come on in."

Evan followed him into the kitchen, tossing his sunglasses onto the counter. "What's up?"

Chris turned back to the jambalaya he was cooking. He had to keep busy. "Cynthia and I had a misunderstanding."

"Don't tell me, she didn't go for all the submission and domination stuff. I thought maybe you'd made some headway because she'd become a little bossier, a little more confident, but I guess I was wrong. There are some women who just don't understand the life and never will."

Even in his maudlin mood, Chris smiled. "Really? Well, what if I told you that about a week ago she took me to her house, tied me down, then fucked my brains out?"

He had the pleasure of seeing Evan at a complete loss for words. He shook his head, and Chris nodded.

"So what's the problem?"

"She didn't want to give it up."

"Give it up?"

"I asked for her submission."

Evan studied him for a moment. "She said no?"

Mentally, he kicked himself in the ass again. Damn, he had wanted her so badly, wanted that concession from her, that he had thrown good sense to the wind. Beneath it all, he knew the reason, but he wasn't about to confess to Evan that he wanted Cynthia to admit she loved him.

Evan brought him out of his thoughts. "So, what happened?"

Chris sighed as he threw the peppers and onions into the heated oil. They sizzled, and a moment later, the scent filled the kitchen. "She asked for time to think. She knew it was coming. All the reading she had been doing, well, there was no way she didn't understand what I was, what I needed. I think I might have rushed it."

Evan was opening his mouth to argue when both of them

201

heard the front door click shut.

Cynthia shut the door with an audible click and sucked in a huge breath. Footsteps sounded against Chris's tiled floor. Licking her lips, she fought the urge to turn and run out the door. The moment he appeared in the doorway to the kitchen, she knew she'd made the right decision. Her stomach flip-flopped, but her heart warmed at the sight of him. The kitchen light poured around him, making it difficult to see his expression in the darkened foyer.

"I didn't know if I would see you tonight."

She could sense the question that lay behind the statement. In his voice, she heard the same worry she felt, and for some reason her own nerves seemed to settle a little. He was dressed in a pair of jeans and a T-shirt, his feet bare. She couldn't take her eyes off him.

She smiled. "You told me to think about it."

He nodded. "What did you decide?"

Her heart melted. The man was too good for her, really. Standing there, a mixture of pride and vulnerability drifted over his face. He had given her more than she had ever given him, in and out of the bedroom. And he had asked this one thing to make them complete. Even with all his bravado, she sensed the undercurrent of fear. And with that, he completely captured her. No one had ever worried about losing her.

She swallowed the lump in her throat and blinked back tears. "What do you think?"

He studied her for a moment. Slowly, sensually, his lips curved. A jolt of heat speared from her stomach to her pussy. Every nerve ending in her body came to attention. Damn, all he had to do was smile at her and she was raring to go.

In two giant steps he reached her. Before she could say a word, she was in his arms. He took her mouth with a kiss so forceful it stole her breath and turned her brain to mush. His hands slid from her waist to cup her rear end. Pleasure burst through her as he lifted her, and she wrapped her legs around his waist.

"I don't mean to intrude..."

Evan's amused voice sounded from behind Chris. Chris broke off the kiss and gently set her on the floor.

"Do you want to do this, Cynthia?" He took her hands in his and raised them to his mouth, placing kisses over her knuckles. "Will you let me share you with Evan?"

She swallowed and looked at Evan. Instead of his usual cynical expression, need and understanding filled his gaze. A tremor of lust danced in her blood, while her heart softened.

"Cynthia?"

She turned to face Chris, the worry in his voice mirrored in his solemn air. Wanting to reassure him, she widened her smile, raising herself to her tiptoes and lightly brushing her mouth over his.

"Yes."

Chris turned to face Evan, who studied the two of them for a second, then came forward slowly. Chris moved behind her, his hands at her waist.

"You do as we say, but you need a safe word, something that you can use to let us know we've gone too far." Evan's voice was low and calm.

Too far. The two words sent a small shard of trepidation into her gut. She wanted to do this, wanted to share this experience, to give and receive. But even as her mind understood that, her heart skipped a beat in fear.

When she said nothing, Chris said, "Any problems?" His breath was hot against her skin, and she could feel his lips brush her earlobe as he spoke.

She wanted this. It scared the living hell out of her and excited her at the same time, but still, she yearned to offer this to Chris.

"You have your safe word?" Evan asked.

She nodded as she watched him. He reached for her shirt, his gaze never wavering from her face.

"Biscuits."

She felt Chris's lips curve. "I like that. Our roles are now reversed, and unless you say that safe word, I have the power. From now on, you answer only when spoken to. Do you understand, Cynthia?"

"Yes."

Chris took over the task of pulling off her shirt. She felt Evan's hands on the clasp of her bra. Both garments ended up somewhere on the floor. Evan's gaze roamed down her body, stopping at her breasts. He brushed his thumb over her nipple while Chris unbuttoned and unzipped her jeans. She'd forgone panties, so within moments she stood completely naked between two fully clothed men.

Chris's mouth brushed her shoulder as he placed kisses leading to her neck. Evan dropped to his knees in front of her, putting him at eye level with her breasts. Both of his hands caressed her as he licked her nipples. The feel of another man's hands and mouth on her breasts should have disgusted her, or at least made her feel nervous. Instead, her hunger grew, her body reacted instantly.

"Ahh, you have such pretty little tits, Cynthia." He took one nipple in his mouth and sucked hard. Chris continued to kiss her neck, but his hands had moved to her ass. His talented fingers drifted over the sensitive skin, sending a rush of heat to her sex.

"Damn, Chris, is she always this responsive?" Without waiting for an answer, Evan shifted to her other breast, pulling her nipple into his mouth, grazing the tip with his teeth.

Chris chuckled. "Always. Isn't that right, baby?"

"Yes." Her voice came out as a whisper. She couldn't fight the craving clawing at her belly as both men slowly caressed her skin. She knew they were building her up to push her to the edge, and God help her, that excited her more.

Evan pulled back from her breast, his breathing a bit labored. She opened her eyes and looked at him as Chris's hands replaced Evan's mouth on her breasts. Her gaze traveled down Evan's body until it reached the bulge behind the zipper of his jeans. She enjoyed a small spurt of triumph at the idea that she'd gotten to Evan.

"You proud of yourself, Cynthia? Really think you're something because you have two men harder than pikes ready to fuck you until you can't walk?" She heard the warning in Evan's voice.

"Yes."

His eyes flared in admiration, and his lips curved. "You no longer hold the Domme role, you are now a sub. Spread your legs. Let me see that pretty pussy."

She hesitated, but not out of fear or embarrassment but in defiance to see how far she could push him.

Chris squeezed both nipples. "Spread your legs for him, Cynthia."

She didn't hesitate this time, but moved her feet out further. Chris pinched one nipple, then the other as a reward. She bit her lip to keep from groaning. Evan ducked his head and leaned closer to her sex.

After taking a deep breath, he said, "Nothing like the scent of an aroused woman. And I like a shaved pussy."

He pressed his mouth between her legs, his tongue sliding down her slit while he inserted one finger into her cunt. As he began to move his finger, he brushed his tongue against her clit. Cynthia almost came then and there, and her knees buckled.

"Now, Cynthia, you know you aren't allowed to come until I say."

Chris's voice was stern, but she couldn't miss that it had deepened, his excitement humming just beneath the surface. His desire became her own, heightening her passion, her pleasure. Evan added another finger and groaned. He pulled back slightly and looked up at her and Chris.

"I think we need to move this to the bedroom, Chris."

She felt Chris nod and Evan stood. As he turned and walked toward the bedroom, Chris moved his hands from her breasts to her waist, urging her forward. It was hard for her to walk since her body was throbbing. Each step was excruciatingly arousing.

Once they reached the bedroom, she noticed that Evan was already undressing. She watched, unable to turn away from the sight in front of her. Chris was gorgeous, the only man she wanted for a lifetime and more. But Evan's body was harsher, his muscles sculpted from his years in construction. She licked her lips when he pulled down his pants and revealed his throbbing erection. A bit longer than Chris's cock, Evan's was not quite as thick. It jutted out from a nest of golden-brown hair, the crown of it purple, with a pearl of cum wetting the head of it. She licked her lips again.

A stinging slap on her rear end broke her attention. It

vibrated down to her pussy. "Don't be bad, Cynthia," Chris said, but she heard the amusement in his voice. He moved from behind her and undressed in record time. Then he held his hand out to her. "Come on, baby."

She smiled at him, and his eyes lit with delight. She took his hand and allowed him to guide her to the bed. He pulled open the drawer to the bedside table, retrieving a set of padded cuffs she hadn't seen before, along with a blindfold.

"Lie down, arms above your head, palms up."

At first, she didn't follow his orders. Not because she didn't want to, but her fear of submitting to him rose unheeded. Would she lose herself again? She looked up at Chris. He waited patiently by the bed.

With a deep breath, she followed his instructions, allowing him to attach the restraints. As soon as Chris finished, Evan placed the blindfold over her eyes, throwing her into darkness.

Panic came first. She didn't like not being able to see what was happening around her. Her pulse scrambled, and her throat started to close up on her.

"Breathe," Evan said. He touched her shoulder, his fingers massaging her tense muscles. "Just let your other senses take over."

She focused on the feel of his gentle touch and the reassuring tone of his voice. Drawing in a gulp of air, she calmed herself and followed Evan's advice. As her heartbeat slowed, her other four senses took over. She felt Evan pull away but she didn't freak out. Instead, she listened to the sound of the two men moving around the room.

"You know the reason for this, of course." Chris's voice was huskier. She curled her toes. The back of someone's fingers brushed the side of her breast. "It will heighten your enjoyment. Taking one sense away allows you to the use the others more.

You still okay?"

She smiled at the worry in his voice. "Yes."

Chris was right. Her sense of smell sharpened. She could even tell the men apart. Evan's scent was enticing, spicy. But Chris's aroused her. It called to her, swept through her blood.

She felt a tongue move over her nipple, and she shuddered. The bed dipped on her left side, where Evan had been standing. He lay beside her, the heat of his body warming her. Nipping at her ear, he rolled her nipple between his fingers, applying just enough pressure. A spark of electricity shot through her veins and she jolted.

The moment she moved, Evan stopped his caresses. "Don't move."

His hard voice washed over her. Absolute authority rang in his tone, but instead of rebelling, it awakened something deep within her. Something that sent heat licking down her spine.

As soon as she settled, Evan resumed his task. He soon replaced his fingers with his mouth, grazing his teeth over the tip of her nipple, then sucking hard as he had earlier.

Chris joined them on the bed. He took her lips in a scorching, wet kiss, even as his fingers danced down her body to her cunt, slipping between her drenched folds. She stiffened as his thumb brushed her clit.

She wanted—no needed—to come. The ache pulsed, her abdominal muscles tightening painfully. Cynthia gritted her teeth and tried to think of something—anything—to keep her from coming.

Lifting his head so his mouth was just a few inches away, Chris said, "Baby. You're so wet." He pressed harder, and tension built in her stomach, heat slipping down between her legs. Another gush of cream filled her pussy.

Just as she reached the point she was sure she would come, Chris pulled his hand away. "Not just yet, *chéri*."

She groaned, although it came out as more of a growl. Both men chuckled appreciatively, but it didn't make them move any faster. She flexed her hands, irritated that she couldn't call the shots. But even as her mind wanted the control, her body was responding. She shivered as Evan's tongue slid along her soaked channel. He murmured appreciatively, the sound sending a vibration to her very core. At the same time, Chris was concentrating on her breasts. His tongue rasped over one nipple, fingers pinching the other. Soon, he had both breasts so sensitive that when he blew on her nipples, she almost came.

With each little lick, each touch, each erotic whisper, they pushed her to the edge of her sanity, ratcheting up the pressure.

"Come on, baby," Chris whispered, his mouth still hot on her skin. "Let go, come for me."

Every molecule of her being insisted on relief, but she couldn't. Something within her held back, something that just wouldn't allow her the relief she needed so desperately.

Evan lifted his mouth away from her.

"You're still trying to control." He let loose a disgusted sigh. "You don't get to choose when you come. *We* do."

Authority threaded his tone. Irritation surged. She opened her mouth to tell him just what she thought of him. But before a word came out, he slapped her pussy. The sting of the smack left her speechless, as did the one that followed. It vibrated deep within her sex.

He blew against her skin as Chris dragged his teeth over the tip of her nipple. One more slap, then Evan set about feasting on her again. His tongue invaded immediately. Cynthia's blood roared in her head, her body taking over, not allowing her mind any control. The muscles of her inner thighs shook, the tremor winding around the pleasure. As Evan added his finger again she felt the control slip from her grip.

Chris moved from her breast, licking and nipping his way to her mouth. "Just let it come, Cynthia."

She shook her head in denial even as pleasure erupted. Her orgasm ripped a scream from her throat. She vaguely registered Chris's crooning approval as Evan shot her up and over once more.

This time, she came with such force that she bowed against Evan's mouth as Chris greedily captured her nipple. Both of the men continued until the last of her convulsions dissolved. She barely registered when one of the men unsnapped a restraint and lifted her off the bed and into his lap. She didn't know who it was until Chris murmured against her ear.

"You did good, baby."

She shivered as the air cooled against her wet skin.

"Not far enough, if you ask me." Disapproval filled Evan's voice, causing her to stiffen her spine.

Chris chuckled. "Don't argue, Cynthia." He stroked his hands up and down her arms, the touch reassuring her. "Evan demands a lot from his subs."

Chris slipped his fingers beneath the blindfold and tugged it off. Even though it wasn't bright, she blinked at being thrust back into sight. The sound of foil ripping told her that Evan was getting a condom ready. He slid onto the mattress and Chris settled her on top of Evan's body. After Chris reattached her cuffs, slipping the strap between the slats on the headboard, he moved behind her. She felt the cool lubricant he worked up her ass to prepare her for his entry.

He removed his finger and stepped away. While he was gone, Evan nipped at her chin, then skimmed his hands across

210

her backside.

"Chris is getting ready, but I want to remind you of the rules." He squeezed her cheeks until she looked down at him. "You have a safe word, be sure to use it if you need to. Do you understand?"

"Yes."

He smiled as he traced one finger between her cheeks. "I knew you'd be fun to have as a sub."

She frowned but before she could respond, Chris slapped her rear to gain her attention. She glanced over her shoulder and smiled.

"Just trying to save you from getting in trouble, babe."

He smoothed his hands over her ass cheeks. She closed her eyes, enjoying the feel of his palms gliding over her flesh, squeezing, teasing. She responded instinctively, as if she had no control over her own reactions.

Chris slipped his hands to her waist, urging her up to straddle Evan. Her sex pressed against Evan's cock and he groaned.

"Damn, you're wet."

She studied his face as Chris continued caressing her skin. A flush lit Evan's cheeks, lust darkened his blue eyes. The bed sagged more, telling her that Chris was moving closer. As his hands left, Evan's replaced them, steadying her.

Panic flashed again, causing her to take huge gulps of air. This was another step she wasn't sure she could take. Excitement intertwined with fear, her brain resisted while her body craved.

Her heart stuttered as she felt the tip of Chris's penis at her back entrance. Evan leaned up and rained kisses over her face as he held her still for Chris's entry. Pain came first as he eased his way in. The initial shock soon melded with pleasure. He'd worked his cock all the way up her ass. Evan shifted his weight beneath her. With a gentleness she didn't expect, he slipped the head of his cock into her cunt. Even as wet as she was, it was difficult for him to enter.

"It's okay, baby, you'll make it."

Chris kept repeating the words but her mind rebelled. His soothing tone did nothing to ease the alarm gripping her. Arousal skimmed over her flesh, fear chilled her mind. She bucked but she was pinned between both men, held captive on the bed.

"Cynthia, please." Chris's breath feathered over her ear. "Let go. This is for you, what you need. I'm here."

Terror fluttered in her chest. She felt Chris's lips against her skin. When he spoke next, his tone had firmed. "There's nothing you can do, nowhere you can go. This is what you want. Just let go. I'm here for you."

She concentrated on his words, listened to his assurances.

"Concentrate on the pleasure. You aren't losing here, Cynthia. This isn't a game."

She stilled but her body shivered with denial. She squeezed her eyes shut, the tears she hadn't known were there rolled down her cheeks. Chris leaned forward and nuzzled against her face.

"This is not about who wins, this is about release, allowing me to take care of you. You need to let your mind take a rest. Your body is telling you what you crave."

She focused on that. The alarm that had frozen her dissolved as the timbre of Chris's words soothed her anxiety.

Both men had held themselves still while Chris calmed her. Knowing what it had cost them, feeling them both throbbing deep within her, she deliberately relaxed.

"That's it, sugar." Evan's voice was almost as comforting as Chris's but arousal had added a rough edge to it. The sound of it danced over her nerve endings, injecting an extra spark to her excitement.

"Ready, baby?" Chris asked.

When she nodded, both men started moving in tandem. As she let her primal senses respond, her hunger grew, her doubts receded. Giving in, allowing Chris to command her to his will wasn't something she was just doing. It was a longing that only he could satisfy. Unbelievably, arousal built again, this time deeper, sharper. Chris and Evan wove a spell of sensuality, drenching her with their passion, their own need to give her satisfaction. All thought disappeared as she gave herself over to the pleasure both men offered her.

Their thrusts increased, the pressure within her built.

"Give over, Cynthia." With Chris's tortured plea, the raw demand spoke to her soul. It was too much to resist and she fell, shattering into a thousand different pieces as her orgasm swept through her. Bliss surged, her body trembling with her release. Just as she started to come down from that first release, Evan groaned, bucking beneath her, pushing her back up into another orgasm, this one stronger than the first. She shuddered as she came. Chris shouted her name and followed her into pleasure.

Chris woke Cynthia slowly, moving his lips over her skin, tasting the sweetness of her flesh. She murmured in her sleep and curled closer to him, the heat of her body warming his heart.

A sense of satisfaction settled within his chest as he scraped his teeth over her bellybutton. When she'd left earlier, he'd been prepared to wait for her, even if it meant forever. She was the one for him and pressuring her would only ruin the act of submission. Now that he could step back and examine it, he realized that his fear had almost driven her away. That it hadn't been some fault in her, but his worry that she would never trust him enough had been his error.

Granted, the result had been a good one. He'd never seen something so beautiful as Cynthia giving in to two men. They'd worn her out, but he knew it was just the beginning. There was more to come before morning.

He felt the bed shift on the other side of her, telling him that Evan had awakened also. A second later, Evan appeared, looking down at Chris.

"Just can't leave her alone?"

Chris smiled up at him. "Can you blame me?"

Before Evan could answer, Cynthia stirred. "Do you know how annoying it is to not only be awakened, but to be awakened by people talking about you?"

Chris trailed his fingers up between her breasts and watched her eyelids flutter, her lips curve.

"I'd say that both Evan and I can compensate you for your discomfort."

"Hmm, you might have a point."

He could hear the smile in her voice and mentally released a breath. He'd worried that she might regret what they'd done, that somehow she'd reject him. She offered him a sleepy grin and cupped his face. He moved up and brushed his lips over hers.

Pulling away before either of them was ready, he groaned his regret. But they had things to do, more steps to accomplish because he was pretty sure after tonight, he wouldn't want to be sharing her with anyone.

Chris looked at Evan, who nodded, knowing what he had in mind.

"Come on, baby."

She stretched, her pretty pink nipples peeking out over the top edge of the sheet. The urge to snuggle under there with her was almost too tempting. But they needed this to be complete.

Chris slipped out of bed, as did Evan. Cynthia sat up, her gaze roaming over his body as he reached for the blindfold. Half aroused already, he didn't even fight the surge of heat that jolted his system, but controlled his expression. The next stage would probably push her further than she expected to go.

Cynthia scooted to the edge of the mattress and stood beside him. He couldn't resist pressing his lips to hers one more time, enjoying the feel of her skin next to his. Her hardened nipples brushed against him and Chris felt his mind melting. Just touching her always affected him this way, and tonight he couldn't seem to control himself.

"Chris." The impatient tone in Evan's voice told Chris he'd waited long enough.

"Turn around," he said and was delighted when she followed his instructions immediately. "Remember your safe word."

Without saying anything else, he covered her eyes with the blindfold once more. He took Cynthia by her hands and set her palms on the mattress. Chris was happy that this time she didn't show any panic. He'd been close to calling the whole thing off when he'd seen her fear when Evan put on the blindfold earlier.

With quick, sure movements, he slipped his hands between her legs and pushed them further apart. He pressed his hand against her pussy. When he felt the damp heat there, he barely resisted the urge to steal more than just a quick feel.

He left her there, knowing she was feeling exposed. They were all unclothed, but without sight, it would add an element of vulnerability. He wanted her submission *and* her trust.

Chris retrieved a riding crop from his bedside table drawer and handed it to Evan, who positioned himself directly behind Cynthia. Anticipation surged and mingled with concern. The last bout had been hard on Cynthia emotionally and mentally. But this time, she needed to believe in him, in their love. She had to give everything over to him without questioning.

Evan raised his hand and brought the crop down on her bare backside. Her gasp of surprise filled the silent room. Her fair skin reddened immediately. Lust crawled along with his nerves, and his cock hardened at the sight and sound when Evan slapped her again, harder.

Evan was known for his way with subs, and he didn't hold back with Cynthia. After one more spank, he slipped the crop between her legs, teasing her cunt. She moved to accommodate him, to rub against the leather to relieve some of the pressure he was sure she felt now. Evan removed the crop.

"I didn't tell you to move."

She stopped. Chris's longing increased tenfold at her compliance. Evan must have sensed his approval because he tossed Chris a frown over his shoulder. He'd shared women with Evan before and knew he was a hardass Dom. Even so, Evan had never crossed the line, and Chris understood he wouldn't this time. But there was always the chance Chris would be too lenient.

With a snort, Evan tossed the crop to Chris and turned

back to Cynthia. He smoothed his hands over her ass cheeks, then up to the tattoo on her lower back.

"This was a bit of surprise." Arousal vibrated in Evan's timbre and Chris noticed the slight shake in his friend's hands. "I wouldn't have expected our magnolia to be so naughty."

He slapped the fullest part of one cheek with his bare hand. Cynthia held herself still, but Chris noted that her breathing had increased and he could smell her arousal. That alone was one of the most erotic things he'd seen. Granted, he'd witnessed Evan work over a sub before, but it had never been his woman, the one meant for him. His heart hitched and skipped a beat. It was a battle to hold onto his control. He wanted to gather her up in his arms, but they weren't done. This had been the easy part.

Evan signaled with his head for Chris to move closer. Drawing in a deep breath, Chris ordered himself to behave and replaced Evan behind Cynthia. Evan handed him a condom and took one for himself. After they'd both put them on, Chris used lube to prepare Cynthia for the next stage.

Again without saying anything, not letting her know who was behind her, he stepped closer and eased his cock into her anus. She stiffened slightly and he paused. His pulse pounded out a rhythm that would surely kill him, but he wouldn't do anything to push her too far. After a few seconds, she relaxed. Joy wrapped around his heart as his blood roared through his veins. He knew it wasn't complete and absolute, but her obedience spoke volumes.

Chris flexed his hips, pushing his shaft further into her small anal opening. She shivered, not from being cold he was sure. She always did that when she was excited. Her excitement spurred his own.

Evan grunted as he settled on the bed next to her. Chris

drew back out and pushed back in as Evan pressed a hand against her pussy. She shuddered again.

To reassure her, Chris brushed his fingers over her hip and left his hand there. As he increased the depth and rhythm of his thrusts, Evan continued to tease her with his fingers and his mouth. She dug her fingers into the bed linens as he felt her body quiver beneath their dual assault.

Soon though, he pulled away, reversing positions with Evan. Chris traced her slit with his tongue as Evan started to enter her from behind. Diving in between her drenched folds, Chris lost himself in the taste of Cynthia. Her muscles contracted against him and he knew she was close.

"That's it, baby." He pressed against her clit, just as Evan smacked her ass. She arched her back, her entire body trembling. Chris leaned up to capture her mouth. Her tongue tangled with his, her hunger easy to taste. "It's okay, come for me."

In the next instant she exploded, jerking with her orgasm as she uttered a scream from her core. A gush of her juice soaked his hand as she continued to convulse.

Evan had pulled out of her by the time she finished. She collapsed on the bed and Chris tugged her into his embrace. Gently, he removed the blindfold and smiled down at her. Several curls clung to her face. Her eyes were closed and her small satisfied smile touched his soul.

It would be easy to lose himself in her pleasure, to just drift with her this way. Two things stopped him. One was the fact that he was far from being satisfied. Two was Evan, who would kill him. The second one made him chuckle.

Chris brushed his lips over her forehead and rolled out of bed. Both he and Evan threw away their condoms then faced Cynthia, who still lay on the mattress.

Since Evan had been more in control before, Chris wanted to be the one calling the shots this time.

"Cynthia, we're not finished."

She didn't say anything but followed their lead and joined them.

Evan opened his mouth, but Chris shot him a look to stop him. His friend was one of the better known Doms in the community, but this was Chris's woman and this was the last of her submission.

"On your knees."

The cold tone he'd adopted was at odds with the heat rippling beneath his surface. She followed his orders without hesitation and his cock twitched. Chris nodded at Evan, who moved in front of her.

Evan took his cock by the base and slid it between her waiting lips. As he jettisoned in and out of her mouth, Chris stepped closer. She closed her eyes and braced herself on Evan's thighs. She moaned, and her pleasure in the act sent primal lust crawling through his veins.

Evan pulled out and Chris said, "Cynthia."

Without missing a beat, Cynthia faced Chris. She looked up at him, her eyes dilated, her skin flushed. She waited there on her knees in front of him. Her breasts rose and fell as her breathing deepened. Her need had been spurred not only by what Evan and he had done to her, but by obeying him.

He slipped his hands through her hair and saw the knowledge in her eyes. She recognized the reason behind her submission, and the ultimate satisfaction she could gain. Delight, love and ecstasy captured his soul, enslaved his heart.

He kept one hand on her head as he guided his cock into her eager mouth. She swiped her tongue against the underside of his shaft before she started sucking. Each time she pulled back, she laved the tip of his penis. She increased her tempo and depth, humming against his flesh. The vibrations from that one little action shifted through his entire body.

Tipping his head back, he closed his eyes and swallowed. His cock bumped against the back of her throat as she took the entire length of him in her mouth.

Sensing Evan's avid attention, Chris opened his eyes and noticed his friend had moved closer.

"Stroke Evan."

As she continued to take him in and out of her mouth, pushing him closer to the edge, Cynthia took Evan's cock in her hand. It only took a few strokes for Evan to come. He shifted closer, taking over her task, and pumped his shaft as he spurted his cum on her breasts. The sight sent Chris hurtling into his own orgasm. She moaned as he came in her mouth, continuing to suckle him until he was spent.

With one last lick, she pulled away and smiled up at him. His hand was still tangled in her hair. He slid it free and cupped her chin, easing her up to stand. She slipped her arms around his waist as he leaned down for a soft kiss.

When he straightened, he noticed the tears rolling down her cheeks.

"Oh, *chéri*." He wiped the tears away with his thumbs. "Don't cry."

She shook her head. "I love you."

He felt his own tears burn the back of his eyes, his knees going weak at the quiet declaration. "I love you too, but why are you whispering?"

"Evan."

He looked up and noticed that his friend had disappeared

and the bathroom door shut. "He left us a moment alone."

Her eyes widened as she looked around. When she turned back to him, she grinned.

The happiness he felt in his heart mirrored in her eyes. "No regrets?"

"Oh, Chris." It was her turn to cup his face, her fingers smoothing over his cheeks. "There can be no regret with you."

As she pressed her lips to his, he felt the contentment he'd craved, the love that he needed, there in her kiss. He snaked his arms around her waist and fell into the kiss.

"You know, if I had seen her first, you would've never had a chance at her."

Chris smiled. "No way. She needed me."

He walked Evan to the door. The first fingers of dawn were creeping over the ocean, but he was ready to have Cynthia to himself. Tonight had been an exercise in submission to two men, but it would be the last time. When she woke up, he wanted to be the only one there.

"I guess there won't be any repeats, from the look on your face."

"Nope. You need to quit running, man."

Evan shot him a look. "I'm not running from anything."

Except the past. Chris let it go, not wanting to ruin the perfect morning. After locking the door behind Evan, Chris hurried back to bed. Throwing his shorts on the chair beside the bed, he slipped beneath the covers and pulled Cynthia into his arms. He sighed as she wiggled her backside against him to get comfortable and then relaxed. As he drifted off to sleep, she whispered, "I love you, Chris."

"I know, *chéri.* I love you, too. Now, get some rest."

Epilogue

One month later

Sweat dripped down Chris's temple as he released a groan. A moment later, he exploded, his body pulled into another orgasm when Cynthia came, her muscles biting down on his cock. Chris pulled the bindings he'd bought earlier that day off her wrists and collapsed on the mattress beside her.

"One of these days, you're going to be the death of me, *chéri*."

She chuckled. "Are you complaining?"

"No. No complaints. Except..." He eyed the digital clock. "You know Max and Anna are landing in about an hour."

"Damn." She jumped out of bed and headed toward his bathroom. "I completely forgot about them."

Chris heard the water start and the shower door slam shut. "Can't imagine how that happened."

He leaned back against the pillows, his muscles relaxed, his body replete. Since the night Cynthia had submitted to him, they'd been practically living together. She was letting Max and Anna stay at her house. Since she'd rented a store for her bakery and was in the middle of redoing the shop, it was easier for the two of them to stay at his place. Her shop was only about a mile from his restaurant.

As he drifted off to sleep, Cynthia's voice drifted out from the bathroom.

"You better get that fine ass out of bed, Chris. I'm not picking them up alone at the airport with these hickeys on my neck."

"No one can see them. They're on the back of your neck."

"And just why did you do something so juvenile?" Her teasing tone made him chuckle.

He didn't answer the absurd question, but did get out of bed. When he reached the bathroom, he opened the shower door.

The water dripped down her body, off her nipples, and bubbles gathered at the apex of her thighs. He smiled at her.

"You start something now, we'll be late."

Ignoring her, he stepped in behind her, slid one hand to cover her breast, another down to her sex. Her body was warm and slick...and his.

He bent his head and kissed the back of her neck. She shuddered in reaction and pushed her ass against his growing erection.

"It's your turn to come up with an excuse," she said.

He chuckled, turning her to face him, then went down onto his knees. "Believe me, I have an excellent excuse."

About the Author

Born to an Air Force family at an Army hospital, Melissa has always been a little bit screwy. She was further warped by her years of watching Monty Python and her strange family. Her love of romance novels developed after accidentally picking up a Linda Howard book. After becoming hooked, she read close to 300 novels in one year, deciding that romance was her true calling instead of the literary short stories and suspenses she had been writing. After many attempts, she realized that romantic comedy, or at least romance with a comedic edge, was where she was destined to be.

She has always believed that romance and humor go hand in hand. Love can conquer all and as Mark Twain said, "Against the assault of laughter, nothing can stand." Combining the two, she hopes she gives her readers a thrilling love story, filled with chuckles along the way, and a happily ever after finish.

To learn more about Melissa Schroeder, please visit www.melissaschroeder.net. Send an email to Melissa at Melissa@melissaschroeder.net or join her Yahoo! group to join in the fun with other readers as well as Mel! http://groups.yahoo.com/group/melissaschroederchat or http://groups.yahoo.com/group/melissaschroedernews for announcements and no chatter.

Desire doesn't care how settled your life is.

Craving Kismet
© 2007 Jamie Craig

Jenny Rohm thinks she has it all—a job she loves, an engagement to her high school sweetheart, a future bright with promise. Then she meets attorney Ashley Edwards and discovers desire doesn't care how settled your life might be.

It starts with a single fantasy. His. Hers. One leads to two, two leads to three, three leads to more. Fantasizing about his wicked mouth or her sinful curves doesn't satisfy either of them for long, though. The more she gets to know him, the harder Jenny finds it to deny the truths Ashley insists on exposing.

The question remains. Is it worth risking everything she has to quench the cravings? Not even Ashley can answer to that. When it comes to what she wants, only Jenny can make the choice.

Warning, this title contains the following: explicit sex, graphic language, anal sex, mild bondage.

Available now in ebook and print from Samhain Publishing.

Enjoy the following excerpt from Craving Kismet ...

Ashley stood outside Jenny's apartment for several minutes, fighting with the instinct to knock on the door again. Bryan wasn't going to wake up. What harm would one kiss do? He just needed to taste her. It wasn't like he was going to fuck her on the bed next to Bryan's unconscious body.

Fuck.

He walked away from the door quickly, trying to will his erection down. Had she been able to sense how much he wanted her? Did she know that nearly every word she said sounded like an invitation to him? Had she been taunting him? Her card burned him through his pocket, and she had just seemed so very...eager.

Except, she wasn't eager. She was engaged. She was just a flirty, carefree, sweet creature who knew how to play nice. That didn't mean she wanted him to slam her against her door and fuck her into oblivion. Even if she flirted back. Even if she offered her card. Even if she drove him to absolute distraction.

Ashley didn't know if he could make it all the way back to his apartment without shoving his hands down his pants, but he intended to give it the old college try. There was the chance that his blood would cool the farther he got away from her. Maybe he wouldn't even need to jack off by the time he got home.

That was too much unfounded optimism.

He was still hard as a rock when he opened his front door.

The table, he decided. Not the door. The table. Over the dinner she made for her fiancé, while he was passed out on the couch. And Ashley had absolutely no ulterior motives for agreeing to take Bryan home instead of just putting him in a cab.

Ashley went directly to the bathroom, shedding his shirt along the way. It would only take a few minutes, and then maybe he'd be able to concentrate on all the work he still had to do.

"And I suppose you think you know what those would be," Jenny dared.

Ashley was certain he knew what would make her happy, what she needed. He licked his bottom lip, his tongue toying with the skin for a moment, attracting her attention. "I know *exactly* what those would be."

Almost lazily, Jenny leaned against the counter, eyes dark and inviting as she set her beer bottle down and out of the way. "One of these days, I'm going to make you put your money where your mouth is."

"One of these days?" Ashley stood, stretching his legs before he approached her. He walked slowly, giving her the chance to bolt if she wanted to take it. "Why not today?"

She never moved. Her eyes never wavered. "Because Bryan's just in the next room."

"He's not waking up. Still..." He touched a finger to his lips. "We'll just have to be quiet."

When he stopped a hair's-breadth away from her, Jenny finally let her sooty lashes dip long enough to glance at his attire and lower. "I'm not really good at being quiet. Especially if you're half as good as you think you are."

"Actually, I've been quite modest." His hands went to her

hips. He moved his mouth over her jaw, never quite touching the skin, as he inhaled deeply. "I'm twice that good. But..." Now his lips skimmed over the same path, a light caress. "I promise, he won't hear a thing."

Her sharp breath was audible, her subsequent exhale warm and ticklish in his ear. She didn't fight the curl of his fingers into the soft denim, but neither did she add to the embrace by lifting her arms and pressing closer. She simply stood there, absorbing the feather kisses along her jaw, her pulse pounding visibly in the hollow of her throat.

"You should stop," Jenny breathed.

"Oh, absolutely," Ashley agreed, the trail of his mouth shifting, bringing his lips closer to hers. He rotated his hips, grinding his hard cock against her, his grip on her tightening. "Make me."

"Stop." Her voice was barely a whisper, and when his mouth skimmed the corner of hers, her tongue darted out to taste him almost delicately. "I mean it."

"Okay," he sighed, before his mouth closed over hers. Her lips were inviting, welcoming, and they parted for him without hesitation. The kiss began slowly, as though he really did think she'd push him away, but soon the pure lust that had been settled low in his gut since he saw her erupted through his body, and the kiss became something harder, more demanding. She clung to his arms, her nails digging through his jacket as he spun her around, backing her up against the table.

Though she tasted faintly of garlic, the beer lent a sweet tang to her mouth as Ashley devoured her, every swipe of his tongue releasing a fresh explosion of flavor that had him hungry for more. Jenny shoved at his suit coat, until only the thin cotton of their shirts separated his hot skin from hers.

She broke from his mouth, gulping for air. "You can't kiss

me forever. And if you make me come, I *will* scream."

Ashley smiled briefly at the challenge, his hands going to her pants. He worked them open with quick efficiency, his lips teasing hers in a series of hard, short kisses. His fingers dipped between her thighs, testing the dampness of her thong, and he knew she was ready for him, perhaps had been since the moment they shut themselves in her tiny kitchen.

Her hands were busy as well. With his jacket gone, Jenny worked at his shirt buttons, pulling them free so roughly that he wondered if he would lose one or two in the process. "Want to feel you." Her nails caught on his bare stomach, scratching up his torso as she pushed the shirt out of her way. "I can't stop thinking about you. You're driving me fucking crazy."

Jenny's hurried words sent a jolt of desire right to his cock, and Ashley knew that he wasn't going to be able to hold off. He wanted her too much; his need was almost palpable between them. He could almost taste it. He kissed her fiercely before turning her around, his hand moving between her legs to spread them apart. She put her hands flat on the table, looking over her shoulder at him with naked longing.

"Are you *trying* to let Bryan know what's going on between us?" she taunted.

Ashley shook his head and tapped his lips again. "Shh." He unzipped his pants, pulling himself out of the constricting material and guiding the head of his cock to her wet heat. Jenny didn't look away as he slid into her, slow, measured, filling her an inch at a time. He didn't want to force a gasp or yelp out of her. Ashley saw the strain on her face as she bit back the moan and knew it was a mere reflection of his own efforts.

LaVergne, TN USA
20 October 2010
201678LV00001B/134/P